WAIF MAID

THE MACMILLAN COMPANY
NEW YORK · BOSTON · CHICAGO · DALLAS
ATLANTA · SAN FRANCISCO

MACMILLAN & CO., Limited
LONDON · BOMBAY · CALCUTTA
MELBOURNE

**THE MACMILLAN COMPANY
OF CANADA, Limited**
TORONTO

WAIF MAID

BY

MAY McNEER

PICTURES FROM WOODCUTS
By LYND WARD

NEW YORK
THE MACMILLAN COMPANY
1930

ACKNOWLEDGMENT

The Author wishes to thank Miss Muriel Ward for devising the melodies which accompany the songs in the story.

CONTENTS

ILLUSTRATIONS

WAIF MAID

CHAPTER I

THE FURY

A STORM, mighty in its intensity, swept through the valley of the Rhine and lashed the quiet river to a foaming fury. The very wolves of the forests cowered in dismay before this wrath of wind and stinging rain, changing to hail as it blew, and the castles on their crags had need of heavy stone and iron bars to hold them steady. Down it roared, bending precious grain to the soil and spilling the juice of wine grapes with a prodigal hand upon the earth. Up again it sailed, and so, crashing and breaking, it gathered the small town of Lutz into its heavy fist and shook from it angrily such of its loose property as might be grasped, painted signs, swinging lanterns, clothes hung out to dry.

The townsfolk, pallid with fear, behind shutters, huddled and whispered intermittently of witches and warlocks and Satan's black hand.

3

"Alack!" they wailed, "there will be no food for us this winter, for we had hardly gotten a bit of a crop going when up comes this tempest to blast our hopes. And it is the third season!"

"But know ye not," muttered an old woman, "that we may yet catch the demon who is the cause of it all. Our brave burgomaster has gone to the fields of Karl the farmer, and with him is learned Doctor Grumchen, smeller-out of Satan's implements, who heard afar of our misfortunes, and came to help us."

The wind rose again to drown their murmurings, and whistled through the country. In the murk of this early autumn day, where a field lay desolate beneath the storm's temper, three figures held their ground, while the voice of one of them came through chattering teeth.

"In faith, goodman, there is nought but the wild wind and the rain, and the rye which bends under them. You have got us here for nothing, with your tales of a witch you have seen running through your fields. A roaring stove and pot of hot wine will put new heart into us. Let us be getting back to the house."

But even as he shouted in the gale the paunchy burgomaster shrank before a blast of blinding wind and hail, and rolled his round eyes fearfully to and fro in the small space left to his vision by the storm. Like an overfed porker dreading the knife he leaned against a straw stack trembling, and groped frenziedly for the muddied black robe of a tall, stern man who stood near him. On the other side, edging close to the stack

as pieces of their shelter were borne wildly up by the angry wind, knelt a heavy peasant, who one moment prayed to the Good God for mercy and the next waved dripping blue-clad arms aloft and shouted vengeance on the baleful cause of his ill luck.

A sudden dazzling flash of lightning ripped the waving curtain of rain as the blade of a cutthroat tears the flesh of his victim.

"Mercy, O Lord, mercy!" shrieked the peasant. Then, when the thunder rolled out, filling their ears, he turned and fled toward his rude home. The burgomaster followed, stumbling and falling and waddling on again, until he dragged his muddied, drenched finery through the door and sank exhausted beside the peasant on the earth floor of the house.

But the lean dark man swayed in the wind, his wild black hair blowing gustily about his gleaming eyes. He seemed to defy the elements to tear him from his work. His dark knotted hands clenched and unclenched; his soaked robe, the fur trimmings dingy with mud, gathered and whipped about his lean black-clad ankles, and his eyes blazing from a set face fathomed the darkness. He turned them expectantly back and forth, back and forth, ever shifting. The storm grew wilder. Large pieces of ice were striking the man. There was a tiny trickle of blood on his forehead. It looked as if the fine point of a knife had somehow drawn blood from weather-stained granite.

Again the thunder roared like a lion, and seemed, this time, to have propelled by its force of sound the immovable figure from its base. The black-robed man leaped forward; in the preceding flash those burning eyes had glimpsed a tiny spot of faded blue, almost hidden under a pile of straw. Fighting his way against the wind, which held him back with a strong arm and tried to snatch the very cloth from his body, he reached the stack and drew from it with a stern hand a small drowned-looking object which clutched to its breast a smaller and wetter black object.

There was a slight smile of triumph on the face of the doctor as he threw the two before him into the hut, and satisfaction lurked, unveiled, in his eyes.

"By the rood of St. Agnes, if 'tis not a maid!" shouted the burgomaster from his position in front of the stove, where he stood absorbing most of the heat into his rolls of fat and his brilliant beribboned clothes. He pushed his long hair, now sadly uncurled, out of his eyes and looked intently at the girl.

"She seems a proper maid," he added, "and stay! Do I not know you, little one?"

"Yea, worthy burgomaster," came the frightened voice of the girl, who, trembling, drew away from her captor toward the protection of a familiar face. "My mother is Frau Muller, of Peterstrasse. We have lived in Lutz for two years agone."

The portly man leaned over in a fatherly fashion and patted the child on her head, but even as he did so he caught sight of the object she held so tightly with one arm. He paled, and withdrew his plump white hand as if he had touched a live coal.

"What be that? Tell me not 'tis a cat, and a black cat too?" He gasped with horror, and turned to the dark man, who stood, triumphant, between the girl and the door.

The peasant was on his knees again in a corner, his booted legs shaking; his shock head moving up and down jerkily.

"Mercy, Lord, O mercy on the poor sinner who has done no harm, who but tries to protect his crops from the hand of the Devil, mercy, Lord, O mercy. I promise two long tapers to the Blessed Lady, come next massday, if this Evil One be driven away. Mercy, Lord, O mercy to a poor sinner who repenteth of the batzen he kept out of his yokel's wages. Mercy, Lord, mercy. . . ." His voice moaned and his under lip flapped as the words stuttered forth.

The burgomaster backed and backed until he almost touched the stove, and his parti-colored finery and drenched plumes sent out an odor of steaming dye.

"Be away, poppet," he shrilled, "be away from me."

"Fear nothing," said the learned man calmly, "I have means to withstand the sins and sorceries of witches. There is nought she can do while I am here, for I have a charmed wafer upon my body."

Suddenly turning to the girl he spoke sternly, with eyes narrowed to slits.

"What is your name, vixen?"

"Elsa Muller, may't please you, sir." She moved farther from him.

"How old are ye?"

"Twelve years, sir."

"Ye are too old to be running wild about fields after a cat.   Why do ye not sit at home, as befits a burgher maid, and learn housewifely arts?   'Tis a bad sign," cried the burgomaster.

"Please sir, I do know housewifely ways.   Ye should see how I can weave and sew and cook a pasty.   But, good sir, in all the town I have no friends but only my mother, and my cat here, who is not afraid of me."

"Ah," puffed the burgomaster, "Sir Grumchen, do ye believe the maid is twelve years old?   She looks not above eight to me, or nine years at most."   He bowed servilely to the dark man.

"Nay," spoke Grumchen, "ye cannot believe a witch maid.   She may be twelve, eight or twenty, and deceiving in appearance by reason of her black arts."

Elsa looked at the learned man in amazement.

The burgomaster had received his cue.   He spoke fearfully.

"Why were you out in the wrath of wind and hail, and you a maid?"

"The Good Lord God forfends me from all evil, and had I done nothing wrong then had I no fear of the Lord's wind and rain, nor lightning nor thunder neither —or so my mother taught me."

"Aha!" cried Grumchen, "an it be her mother, burgomaster!   Your trip with me into the tempest has not been in vain.   She whom you seek is here in your own town."

"Mercy, Lord, O mercy," came the sound of the chattering peasant from his corner, while the fatty substance before the stove quivered like a jelly and shook his colored ribbons, as he crossed himself piously.

"Is it not strange that she should be unafraid of such a tempest, burgomaster?"

The fat man nodded emphatically.

"Is it not more strange that she carries under her arm one of the instruments which Satan gives a witch to work her evil deeds?" He pointed to the shaking kitten, which stared at him with frightened blue eyes.

"But, sir," cried the girl, "'tis my friend and comrade and 'tis she who made me run into the fields and be caught in the storm there, for she ran from our home and I was much afeared for her life when the wind came up so mighty. When I had found her we hid beneath a straw stack till the storm might abate."

"Ah! An did ye not dabble your hands in the brook before the tempest came down so heavy?" hissed the fat man.

"I but washed my hands there once, to loose the stains of mire where I had stumbled and fallen after my katze, who led me a merry chase, the popinjay." And Elsa laughed gayly.

But the light-hearted laughter sounded strange in that dark, smoked room, where the storm still beat without, though with bated fury, and the choppy voice of the peasant ran on like a night insect from a corner. The witch hunter's eyes narrowed slitwise.

"An did your mother teach you to dabble your hands in brooks, and to say devilish words over it?"

"Why yea, she did always teach me to be cleanly."

"'Tis proof, sir," came the oily voice of the burgomaster.

"Sith, I like it not," he added, "an I like not staying in the same hut with the vixen."

"To town with her," said Grumchen, grasping Elsa by the arm; and to the prattling peasant, "Get back to work, goodman. We shall have no more tempests now."

The rain and hail had almost ceased, and the wind was blowing itself out futilely against the upper hills. The air smelled fresh, laden with odors of wet grain and burst grape. Elsa rubbed her kitten dry as she sniffed the wind and walked beside the doctor. The burgomaster puffed along in front of them, his fear decreasing and his importance growing with each step which took him nearer the town and his prideful office. He furtively twisted his stringy curls as he went, loath to appear before admiring subjects with lank locks.

Heads were craning from tiny windows and less timid folk were emerging into the narrow streets as this small procession entered. A child ran, laughing, pursuing a waddling goose across their path, but he turned and fled with a wail of fright to his mother's voluminous skirts as he caught the black eye of Grumchen.

The burgomaster started into the center of town,

to his hall, but was recalled suddenly by the stern voice of the witch hunter.

"Not to the Rathaus, master! Know ye not that the mother will escape on a broomstick an she gets wind of this before she can be taken?"

"But what to do then, sir? We cannot take her. There must be armed men and a basket."

"Then will I go to her house and hold her with my charms while you get things necessary. But be not long."

Bowing low to the intrepid man the burgomaster scuttled around a corner and was gone. Gripping the girl a little tighter, Grumchen advanced toward Peterstrasse which was on the edge of town, near-by. Elsa's heart throbbed violently as she saw a curious crowd collecting around them. There was a great fear of she knew not what growing with each moment. She clutched her small companion tighter and walked along beside the tall man striving to keep pace with his lengthy strides.

Up a steep hill they climbed until they reached a tiny house, perched at the very top, with its over-hanging gables almost touching its neighbor across the street. They stopped on the cobble stones beneath. Looking from a small window on the first floor was the calm, surprised face of Elsbet Muller.

The door opened under her hand as she bowed the man into her front room, and bade him be seated on a settle beside the tall tile stove. But he would not sit. He stood between the two and their door, and seemed

to defy the powers of the foul fiend himself to move
him from that place.   His eyes burned fiercely.   He
looked intently at Elsa's mother.

"Whence came ye, woman?"

"From the mountains, sir, and before that, when
my husband was alive, from Dresden town.   But that
was eight years agone, we left there."   She sighed.

The man drew his brows sharply together.   His
eyes narrowed.   From the slit between his lids came
a sudden gleam of triumph.   Elsa, seeing this, recoiled.
She thought of the savage, gleeful eyes of a wild dog
she had once seen seize upon a piece of meat dropped
by a butcher boy.

Grumchen pointed a bony finger at Elsbet Muller.

"Woman," he cried, "deny not your guilt, for we
have taken your child in the act of witchcraft, and it
is well known that no child can practice the evil arts
unless taught by her witch mother."   The woman's
quiet face was frozen with amazement, which changed
to fear as she saw the man's eyes.

"Alack, sir!" she asked, "how could ye have taken
my Elsa in such practice?   Never has she been aught
but a good girl and well versed in pious ways.   And
I . . . oh, sir, I be not a witch.   Sooth 'tis against the
kindly thoughts of God to believe in the black arts."

"So ye believe not in them!   All real witches say
so, I ween.   'Tis more proof."

Frau Muller drew Elsa protectingly to her, and with
an arm about her daughter's shoulder she stood in
rigid anxiety.

"Alas, I know not what to do," she murmured. "But my neighbors will clear me, for no one can say that I have injured mankind, cattle, nor the good grain and fruits."

"Then will I have them in," said the man coldly, and in truth that was an easy matter, for the neighboring housewives had gathered before the house, peering and whispering and shaking their heads. The doctor opened the door and let them file cautiously in. They grouped, with a stiff rustling of skirts, on the opposite side, across from Elsa and her mother, and carefully left a wide space of worn board between.

"Hausfrau," came the man's metallic voice to a stout, loquacious woman, "have you aught to say against this vixen, who is undoubtedly a witch? Have you any crimes to declare against her?"

Dead quiet for an instant, then the excited woman's voice:

"Welladay, good sir doctor! I would like to be silent as was Mumchance, who was hanged for saying nothing, but in sooth I have had so much trouble lately in my dairy that I have known for long that my cows were bewitched. And alack, my two best ones! They have not given the milk they should, and who but a witch could work such misfortune. I know nought 'gainst Frau Muller, but she has been in Lutz only two years. We have not heard her say aught of her life before she came." She spoke suddenly in a lower voice, turning her eyes fearfully toward Elsa's mother. "She passed my barn but yestreen, for I saw her, and who knows how many times she may have been within?"

"And I," called a lean sour woman, "I live but across the way, and look you, did not my pig, that was so fine and plump, die last week?" She folded her hands in her apron and drew her lips to a thin line.

"And my little Franz did get a pox on him some weeks agone, and was only saved through the intercession of our Blessed Lady."

"And my goodman's grain was blasted with a blight in its prime, before even the storms came to wipe it away."

"And my cream did all turn to sour when the Devil's thunder hit the town."

Elsa looked up into their faces with astonishment. She knew that the women disliked her mother for being a stranger who kept her own council, who could read, and who never mixed much with them or gossiped on the doorstep. For verily the goodwives' tongues seemed tied in the middle and wagging on both ends.

Elsa thought of the times she had run away in distress because she had overheard some careless comment on the strange habits of Frau Muller. She turned a scared face to these neighbors now, and saw their eyes, round and glassy with sudden suspicion, fixed on her mother. On the other side were the dark, flaming pupils of the witch hunter, alive in the rigid mask of his countenance. Elsa shrank against her mother, who stood stiffly, with head held high. Grumchen wheeled around and bade Frau Muller answer the accusations. Then Elsa heard her mother's voice.

"Have you no kindliness, that you accuse me so unjustly? You, Frau Weber, do you turn against me too?" She looked despairingly at a gentle woman who had said no word in all the confusion.

"Fain would I be shut of this," she murmured. "I have had some ill luck with my fowls of late, but I accuse not Frau Muller, for never, since she came to our Lutz has she done aught, to my knowledge, that was unkindly."

"You would be clement, good Frau Weber," said Grumchen, "but it is well understood by a man who has learned the vile ways of Satan and his witches that your fowls did not die a natural death. And you," looking intently at Elsbet Muller, "how did your husband die? Why came you here?"

"He was a good burgher. He told me to come to Lutz when he was no more, for it was in this town he had left his father long ago. Alas, when I came his father and all his folk were dead, but I stayed, for it was the childhood home of my husband."

"How do we know but what she was driven from that place as a witch; how do we know but what her evil charms killed her husband?" cried the man.

"But, sir," declared Frau Weber, curtsying, "what she speaks must be truth, for my father knew Herr Muller, the father of her husband."

"That proves nothing. The Evil One often leavens

a lie with a bit of truth to gull the righteous.   In what way did your husband die?"

"Good sir," answered Frau Muller in a low, sad voice, "he was killed by thieves who entered our home by night."

"Ah," cried the man somberly, "methinks there be other reasons why.   To the Rathaus with her for trial."

"Short shrift she will get," whispered the stout woman, as they all drew their skirts from Elsa and her mother.

"Do but see," shrilled a housewife, "she does not weep.   A witch cannot shed tears, an that you all know."

"Yea," answered Grumchen, "for tearful grieving, weaving and deceiving are suitable to women, but a witch is no longer a woman."

"Good sir," said Elsbet Muller in a calm but despairing voice, though she was pale as death, "do but allow me to go to my chamber and get my mantle."

"Nay, woman.   Ye pass not from this room, for well I know that ye keep black charms in that chamber of yours, whereby ye may do mischief to these true folk."

"Why do ye seek to do me and mine harm, and we have never before set eyes on ye?"

"Woman," said the man coldly, "it is my life business to go about scenting out witches, whose ways I study, for the good of the lives and property of these good folk."

Elsbet Muller stared straightly a long time.

"Nay," she murmured calmly, "there are other reasons too, I believe.   There are other reasons than good will to folk."

The lean man raised his fist suddenly, angrily, then dropped it swiftly.

A clang of metal was heard on the stones outside. The learned doctor stepped from the doorway.   Six sheep-faced soldiers clanked into the little room and uneasily ranged themselves around Frau Muller.

"One moment," she begged, "what is to become of my little girl?   Will you let her have this house and the property in it, which does rightfully belong to her?"

"Not so.   The property of a witch be forfeited. And as for the girl, we know well enough what to do with the daughter of a witch."

"May the God of the innocent protect her, and may you live to rue this day!"

The man's arm shook.   "Seize her!   Where is the basket?"

"Here it be, noble sir, here it be," the oily voice of the burgomaster issued from the door, where he stood like a fat and gaudy parrot.   He waved his plushy hand grandly toward an urchin who carried on his head a withe basket of enormous size.

"The witch basket!" whispered the stout neighbor.

"Put her in," commanded the witch hunter, as the boy crawled out like a snail leaving his shell, and turned the basket over on the floor.   "And let not her feet touch the earth between here and the Rathaus, for if, mayhap, she can get her wicked foot on ground she will call around her instantly the devils of thunder and lightning, who can, for all our protective charms, slay us and set her free to ride into the air in a brimstone cloud.   An if, by luck, she cannot do that, still by putting foot to earth she may secure the stubborn gift of silence, or denial, which makes so hard the work of gaining repentance from a witch."

"Ye do not need to put me in," murmured Frau Muller, slowly, "for if, methinks, I must die, I be ready.   But for my little Elsa I could not wish to live." Turning swiftly she pressed her daughter to her, and as Elsa's arms clung frantically around her neck, she whispered,

"My dear one, do ye take care of yourself, and stay not till ye are in Nürnberg with your father's kinsman."

Elsa could not see the room through her tears, but her mother's face seemed suspended in a mist before her.   The woman stepped dazedly into the basket and seated herself there.

Elsa swayed forward, then with a face of agony, she jumped to the man and seized his bony hand, which he snatched from her as if she carried the black death.

"Sir," she cried, "we have had nought to do with the Evil One, but you . . . you are the Devil himself!"

A dark crimson tide mounted to the peak of black hair above the eyes of the witch hunter.   He turned with a semicircular motion and slapped Elsa across the face, flinging her upon the floor. She saw a long black robe above soft pointed shoes, self a face convulsed with rage. Two black eyes blaz down. She gave a low cry.

The soldiers bore their burden into gaping streets, where townsfolk crossed themselves fearfully.

Elsa ran to the window, and, from far down the street, her mother's eyes, hopeless, pitiful, met hers for one brief moment. The girl gave a low moan, like a small soft animal wounded by a swift arrow, and crumpled upon the floor, where she beat her head on hard boards.

A small sound roused her. Frau Weber came in through a tiny door at the rear, and touched the girl gently. She stood and obeyed, in a stupor, the kind hand.

CHAPTER II

THE WORLD IS SO WIDE

In the narrow quiet of cloistered halls nuns, swinging black robes as they walked with steps firm and
purposeful, smiled softly at the ecstatic faces of young
novices in white who passed them with reverent bows.
The novices, some of them scarcely more than children, performed their duties, intoned their prayers,
and fingered their rosaries with strict fidelity, and
with eyes on the earthen floor.   But once and again
one of them, not yet entirely disciplined in convent
ways, looked with pity on the sad white face of Elsa,
who abode among them but was not of them.   They
were good to her, those who noticed her, and treated
her with remote gentleness and pity, as did the nuns.
All but Sister Ursula.

In the land of the Rhine there was no sister so
devout and stern as Sister Ursula.   She lived only for
prayer and meditation and strict discipline of the flesh.

22

Her self-punishments were the he   st undergone b
anyone in the convent because   -imposed, an
was no less strict when called upon to set
other sinners.   It was her eye which foll   Elsa,
as she helped with duties of the clois   .nd it
was Sister Ursula who always inspir   with
fear.

The stern, tall woman had a w   ping Elsa
as she walked timidly through th   and asking her
if she had yet repented of her s   destroying the
crops of the farmers and in mixing in the arts of the
Evil One.   Elsa could only stammer and look at her
with a more frightened eye, and run off to hide her
face in the thin coverings of her small cell bed.   Elsa
began to dream of the witch hunter, with his burning
black gaze, and sometimes his face changed to the
white, stern expression of Sister Ursula.

The nuns set her many prayers and fasts, so that,
when she was not on her knees in her bare cell or before the altar in the small gloomy chapel she was sitting alone, thinking how much she wanted to return
to her home, to that life which was now a dream.
Elsa grew steadily thinner and whiter, until one day,
when she sat in the convent garden listlessly, she saw
the kind face of Sister Charitas looking down at her.
The nun seated herself beside the girl and patted her
hand.

"Child," she said softly, looking around as if,
strangely enough, she did not wish her fellow nuns
to hear her words, "this life does not agree with ye

well.   Tell me, hast any desire to become a holy sister
here?"

"No," murmured Elsa timidly, seeing the pitying
face, "I like it not.   I reverence the good sisters, but
I have no wish to be one of them."

"Then tell me," whispered Sister Charitas, "if there
is aught I can do to help you?"

"Alas," said Elsa, "they have taken my mother from
me.   Since Frau Weber hid me here I have always
been afeard I may be found.   And ye have even shut
my friend, Fräulein Bach, away from me among the
pots and pans, and will not let me see her, saying that
it is not meet for a girl soon to be a novice of the convent of St. Clare to love a cat.   Ah, and I miss her
sorely."   Elsa dropped her head suddenly and the good
Sister Charitas saw a big round tear fall on the coarse
cloth of the girl's convent dress.

"Child," she asked abruptly, "have you a human
friend anywhere who would look out for you, could
you but reach him?"

"Yea, sister, there is a distant kinsman of my father's in the town of Nürnberg.   He has a great brood
of his own, but he would not let me go hungry, and
mayhap I could help his wife in the kitchen."

"'Tis well then.   I will see that you get to him.
Stay, there is an honest carter going that way with
a load soon.   He brings supplies to us here to-day.   I
shall see him, an if he be not willing to take you, then
will I get another.   Sister Ursula must not find me
out in my schemes for you, for she would not let you

go, but I do hold with the belief that it be a sin to keep ye here so close to Lutz when there is danger of Grumchen finding ye out. And," she added, looking about her still more fearfully, "I strongly doubt me that a gentle girl such as you could have dabbled in the works of the Foul Fiend, but say not that I said so.

"And," she continued gently, "I doubt too that I should send a little maid out into the world alone, but 'tis better so than that she should be found here. I greatly fear for your health too, child. These long fasts that Sister Ursula puts upon you, while good for your soul, will not keep your body with us much longer an ye do not improve mightily.

"Now go in and pray to the good Saint Elizabeth, who protects gentle maidens, and to the Blessed Virgin, to have you in their keeping. And be ready at cockcrow, before the first light, but do not set a flame to your taper. An I will come to you." She turned abruptly and walked away, but Elsa, whose whole face lighted with joy, caught her by the gown.

"Good sister, can you not find me my Fräulein Bach, for I must not leave without her?"

"There, child, I shall try. Go to your prayers now."

Elsa turned and ran into the cool, shadowed building, and, trembling, fell on her knees in her own cell, where she raised supplicating hands to gentle St. Elizabeth.

There was not much sleep for Elsa that night, since fear that she might not awaken in time startled her

eyes open frequently. The hours seemed each as long
as a lifetime, and when she heard her door creak open
gently she had given up, in despair, any idea of ever going to seek her mother, or even of ever seeing Fräulein
Bach again. She was sobbing quietly on her pallet
when a thin streak of early dawn light filtered through
the opening door, and she saw, fearfully, a dim shape
standing there.

"Child, child, up, for an ye be going ye must go at
once."

Elsa sprang to the sister, and the nun noticed that
the girl had slept fully clothed. Hastily throwing a
cloak around her, Sister Charitas thrust at Elsa a small
bundle of food wrapped in her faded blue cloak, which
had been taken from her, and a warm bunch of black
fur. With a murmured prayer for her safe-keeping,
the nun pushed the little girl into the hall and through
a door which opened to the sky. Leading her silently
through the convent garden the sister fumbled in her
gown and drew forth a key, with which she opened,
not without some difficulty—for the tiny door was
long unused—a passage into the world. Elsa stood
a moment silently, then drew one arm around the good
sister's neck, and thanked her chokingly.

"There, child, thank me not, for I can only hope
I have done rightly by you after all. Now go. Make
haste!"

She turned and was folded into the black shadows of
the garden. The door creaked shut. Elsa looked
around her, wiping her eyes, at ghostly shapes of trees,

just coming into view with the first faint opening of day.

"Do as the saintly sister bade you, little one," said a gruff voice behind her. Elsa jumped nervously and clasped her kitten closer. "And make haste," continued the voice; "come this way to the cart."

Elsa saw then, close by, a wagon with rudely cut wood wheels, packed high with goods of some bulky sort, which were covered against the weather by heavy cloths. Guided by the carter's hand, she climbed into the vehicle, and squirmed through a hole between sacks, which the man pointed out to her, until nothing of the girl was visible and she could lie there, with but a tiny slice of sky in her sight. It gave her a little comfort to get out of the convent gown and into her old blue dress once more, though the changing was a difficult feat among the sacks.

Onward they jogged, and as they moved slowly Elsa settled Fräulein Bach into a more comfortable curve of her arm, wrapping her around carefully in her mantle, whispering to her friend her thoughts.

"The carter will, of a surety, Fräulein, take us through Lutz, or near there, where they are keeping mother, and we shall slip through this hole to find her there. Do you not think we can find her, if we search through all the town? But we will have to hide from the dark one, who thinks we must needs be witches, the three of us. Ah, Fräulein, do you not wish we were again in our home on Peterstrasse, with our comfortable house and our mother? Ah, I am sorry now that I minded her not when she told me to mend my saffron kirtle neatly, and I did but hide it behind a chest, for I was of a slothful mind."

Elsa buried her face in the black kitten's fur and cried again, while her two yellow braids jerked in rhythm with her sobs. But she halted suddenly at the words of the carter, who, after the habit of men who ride much alone, was conversing to himself in an amiable spirit.

"Almost to the town, an a good glass of ale would fit my throat as a pair of red shoon fits the toes of a maidservant on a holiday. But the pious Sister Charitas bade me not enter Lutz, but go straight by road to meet the other wagons on their way to Nürnberg, and say nothing of the maid till far from here. These do be five good pieces of silver she gave me, an strongly tempted am I to wet my gullet with one of them. But nay, I dare not, for all powerful be these saintly sisters, an she hear of it a plague might fall on me for my broken promise. Welladay, 'tis not so far to the next town, where I do meet good Johannes and his fellows, and may the saints forfend me against thieves till I get there." His ruminations died off in a mutter.

Elsa lay a moment quiet, then clutched the Fräulein as she whispered:

"Fräulein, dost think we can pass the town of Lutz with no word of our mother? Methinks it may be dangerous, but we must out from here when we get nearest the place where they keep her."

Hardly able to stay quietly among her sacks she yet managed to contain her impatience until her small slice of sky grew brilliantly blue, and she could see the sunlight of late morning slanting through her corner. Silently she pushed and shoved the yielding bags of grain until there was an easy hole to slide to the road behind the cart.

"Now can ye but be quiet, Fräulein, we may yet escape, but if ye let out one tiny squeak we cannot. So do ye remember that." The kitten, purring softly in its warm corner of the cloak, said nothing, but looked at Elsa intently for a second, then solemnly blinked both eyes. That the girl took for an answer, and so, relying on it fully, she began, as soon as she recognized the surrounding territory, to edge from her nest. The kitten came too, as needs must with a tight small hand grasping her close, but her purring ceased and Elsa held her breath. Farther and farther out they slid until the road below moved along directly under their eyes. Fortunately the old horse was slow, and the loquacious carter himself filled his ears with so much noise that they were deaf to any sounds behind him.

Plop, they landed in the mud, and as they picked themselves up ruefully they saw, Elsa with relief and the Fräulein with large-eyed indifference, the cart withdrawing itself gradually from their sight. And the Fräulein, with entire thoughtfulness, was after all to be depended on, for she made not a sound. Elsa brushed off what mire she could from her long skirt,

and gathered the kitten under her cloak, for it would
not do to be seen with her.

"Tell me, Fräulein Bach, why do the good sisters as
well as the people, think evil of ye?   It is a beautiful
black coat ye wear, and makes me think not of evil.
But ye do be filled with mischief, and so, though ye may
struggle, I shall not put your feet on earth, for in
trice ye would be off leading me another chase across
the fields.   And to-day we must look for our mother."

So townward she trudged bravely, with feet sticking
in the mud and cloak drawn close about her.   In the
distance, there was the carter moving farther and farther away, but with a woeful face turned toward the
taverns.   Presently Elsa lost him from sight entirely,
and discerned smoke rising slowly from the chimneys
of Lutz.   Her heart was gladdened by sight of familiar
copse and meadow and hill when, at the top of a steep
ridge, she looked down on the pointed roofs and
painted house fronts of her town.

"Whence come the crowds, Fräulein?" she murmured curiously, noticing that the narrow cobbled
streets were filled with a mob of chattering, laughing,
gesticulating folk, in crimson, blue and rainbow hose
or farthingales.   But Fräulein Bach only wrinkled
her short black nose under the mantle, and stared
solemnly.   Elsa sat down to rest a few moments, and
then, remembering her quest, jumped to her feet and
started for the town, where the crowds, she thought,
would keep her from being recognized until she was
again at home.

"It must be a feast day, Fräulein," she whispered,
"for peasants from all the country round are here.
In truth it be a goodly crowd." But by this time
Elsa was hungry, for she had eaten nothing all day,
and the day had been a long one. So she found a
sheltered doorway, which turned at an angle from
‸   .treets, and ate of the bread and cheese given her
y pious Sister Charitas. Fräulein Bach too ate of
the food, and seemed to find the cheese good.

Rising with fresh courage Elsa again concealed her
comrade and found her way by side streets to Peterstrasse. But when she reached her home there was no
open window, and no latch out on the door. The
house was closed, its shuttered eyes withdrawn from
the busy life about it. It turned a forbidding, un-
recognizing face to the girl's grief. Elsa went sadly
away to wander aimlessly, peering into windows,
through doorways, trying to discover by some word,
some chance phrase or some glimpse a trace of her
mother. But she was afraid to ask, and if she saw
a familiar head she dodged away from it.

Early afternoon found her wearily walking the
streets, not knowing quite what to do, and holding
the kitten with difficulty, for the Fräulein had a strong
desire to run about and objected to being held beneath a dark cloak, when sunlight and such fascinating
objects as blowing leaves and scampering mice were of
a surety almost within reach of her paws.

So, when the kitten gave an angry squawl, Elsa had
to run away from a group of prattling folk and hide

in the nearest doorway. Once or twice she caught
a glimpse of a black velvet robe which threw her heart
into her mouth, and caused her to cringe fearfully behind refuse with which some streets were littered.
All day she wandered thus, not daring to come out
and ask, but hoping by edging close to crowds to hear
of the whereabouts of her mother.

When dusk drew upon the town and even pigs were
gathered into outhouses by their irritated owners,
Elsa, tired and discouraged, had heard nothing of her
whom she sought. She was afraid to approach the
town hall. Suddenly she saw a number of men and
women, followed by beggars in tattered rags, and
street urchins running madly, some falling, some shouting, toward the market square. There was a hushed
roar of voices too. Elsa stumbled with them, as fast
as her tired feet could carry her, and she was vaguely
conscious as she ran that her stomach clamored for
food. But still she ran until she stopped at the edge
of a mob that filled the market place with excited
babel of sound. In the center she could just discern,
by standing on tiptoe, a heavy wooden stake. It was
evidently around this that the people circled, but she
could not push closer.

"Away with the witch!" cried a voice near-by, and
Elsa paled and trembled.

"She poxed me with a plague!"

"She lamed my horse!"

Elsa shook violently, but, strive as she might she
could get no closer. Beggars in foul garments, wear-

ing filthy curls, with cast-off hose and dirty, ragged doublets slashed in many faded colors, which once had fitted the dignified forms of wealthy men, jostled her rudely, craning their necks to see the excitement. But there were others than beggars and thieves in that mob; Elsa could distinguish the neat, gay clothes of good burghers, and even the kirtles of their wives, and these were just as eager for a sight of the stake as the rascals. The girl turned blindly and saw suddenly, through a gap in the throng, a piece of blue cloth that looked vaguely familiar to her.

Was that her mother's dress? Elsa drew herself as high as she could by dint of standing on her toes, and stared hungrily through the forest of moving heads. There was a deafening noise of shouting. As the heads shifted and turned, seeking a better view, the girl for a brief instant peered through a small opening between them and saw a familiar, rigid face. She reeled back out of the crowd and leaned against a doorway.

Suddenly everything became dark, black as the depths of a forest, and she fell in a limp heap in the shadows, while the Fräulein, frightened at so much noise, crouched behind her.

When Elsa opened her eyes she felt, before she saw, that something strange had happened to her. She seemed to be lying stretched out on two strong bands, with space all around her, and darkness lightened by a feeble gleam coming indistinctly from before her. She was moving, yes, she was certainly moving along, for steps seemed to jog, and every once in a while stumble, beneath her. She opened her eyes and stared up into the shadowed face of a man, whose fruitful crop of whiskers covered all of his countenance save only a turned-up nose and a pair of very bright blue eyes. A cap hid his forehead, and as he walked he nodded solemnly. But whenever he stumbled, as happened frequently in that dark and ill-paved thoroughfare, Elsa heard his hoarse voice rumble internally and mutter under his breath. She was frightened, but, lo ...g 'n at the bright blue eyes, she ceased to be alarmed. hither she was being carried she knew not, but neither did she fear. She was so tired, so very tired. And as she closed her eyes again, with a dim remembrance of big arms and a hairy face, and those blue eyes, and the sound of footsteps about her, she fell into a heavy sleep.

CHAPTER III

THREE AND ONE MAKE FIVE

ELSA sat up and looked with a bewildered gaze at a curtain of dark green leaves, which shut her in as if she were a forest elf. "'Tis a dream," she thought, "for this could not be real." Above her she could just see a small square of cloudy blue, the cool color of early morning. She turned her head in astonishment and noticed how a sunray pushed pale gold fingers through the foliage. With a rush of memory, her face trembled like a small rabbit's, startled, rigid with fear, defenseless and alone. Her mother was gone! In all the world there was no one so lonely as she. The great, mad roar of a mob filled her ears and drummed ceaselessly behind her eyeballs. She knew not where she was.

There was a feeling of some other presence behind her, but terror stiffened her neck. With an immense effort the girl turned her head. Three men sprawled

beside the dying embers of a big fire, which still smol-
dered darkly in the crisp morning air.   At a little distance were carelessly thrown three stout wood staves.
What strange men were these?

Elsa fixed her eyes, fascinated, on the nearest, a
small round man, who wore a soiled suit of green, a
monstrous pair of boots and a blue cloak which spread
widely on the ground about him.   He looked up
swiftly, with a bird-like turn of his bald head.

"Welladay!   The maid awakes.   'Tis time we made
ourselves known to her."   He bounced to his feet and
bowed deeply, with a wide sweep of his arm.

"Fräulein," he cried, "I be your humble servant,
Werner, of the gracious city of Mainz.   My talents lie
in so many directions that to consider each would make
you as dizzy as the flagellant who lashes himself
bloody for his soul's sake.   And by the feet of St. Anthony I am glad that I have not that kind of soul.
But my chiefest virtue, aside from a handsome appearance, charming speech, a witty tongue, a hearty appetite and a kindsome disposition, lies in my music.
For know ye that I was once a poet-musician of the
best, now, alas, much fallen in fortune and reduced
to traveling with these unrefined churls you see."

Elsa trembled and shrank from the queer speech.

He flourished his arm toward a huge fellow dressed
in a worn doublet, with red hose and a blue cap which
matched his bright solemn eyes in color.   His beard
was shaggy.   Yet, those were, undoubtedly, the same
curly whiskers of the dark night before, and those must

be the two strong arms which had carried her from the town.   The big man sat bolt upright with no support for his back, which, withal, needed no support, for it was as straight as a broad arrow.   His feet, in soft, pointed shoes with heavy sandals strapped beneath, extended stiffly before him on the ground.

"Here," shouted the fat man, "is he who was your coach and horse yestreen.   His name be Hans, of Strasbourg.   Trust not his simple and honest countenance, for he hides a store of blasphemous oaths beneath that hairy copse, albeit they only emerge in rumbles.   And the sounds he draws from yon zinck," pointing to a straight tube-like musical instrument which hung from a leather band about the neck of Hans, "are enough to slay ye out of hand!"

A deep rumble, as of a turbulent river within a cavern, issued from the throat of Hans.

"Forbear, Werner, ye will scare the maid."

Elsa saw that he looked at her gently from his porcelain-blue eyes.

"This gallows tree," cried the fat man, waving his pudgy hand grandly toward a long lanky fellow whose stringy black hair fell into sad eyes as he lay on his back with arms spread wide and an expression of complete oblivion, "this gallows tree, and methinks the gibbet may seize its own yet too, this gallows tree which you see spread upon earth, is our energetic Melchior.   He carries the dudelsack."

Elsa's eyes followed dazedly the fat finger, which pointed to a big affair consisting of a leather bag with queer pipes attached, the top decorated by a carved head of some hideous creature, whether woman or animal she could not tell.

Werner, with a grin at the girl's astonishment, waved his arm again toward the bagpipe upon the grass, as he continued:

"And, with much persuasion, Melchior has even been known to draw forth sounds from this instrument which set cows to bellowing and little children to running in to their mothers shrieking of the Black Fiend, who boils infants and feeds the soup to witches, and who but now plucks out sounds from a foul contrivance built by devils in the smoking pit."

Elsa listened, shrinking farther and farther from the gesticulating speaker; and as he reached the end she sprang up in terrible fright and ran shakily through dense undergrowth, which scratched her face and hands until the blood came, fighting her way out. But behind her there was a rumble from Hans, the bearded one, growing into a roar at Werner, who capered about in anguish at the result of his careless words. Hans crashed into the bushes and gently touched Elsa, who lay, sobbing violently, in a small patch of grass.

"Nay, nay, little maid. Be not afraid, for Werner's words are as the barking of a yapping dog, all noise and no venom. Come back to our sheltered place. Be not afraid."

Elsa looked up at him and took sudden confidence. She rose and made her way behind him to the fire.

"Alack, may the fiends attack me, and tear me limb from limb, if I be not the sorriest vagabond to frighten a small maid so!   Devil take me, and fly away with me to the hottest flames."

"Werner," shouted Hans in a rage.   "Hold your clack!   Don't ye see ye are making things worse with the Fräulein.   Come," said the big man gently to Elsa, "are ye not the daughter of Frau Muller, of Lutz?   I thought I recognized ye on the step last night."

Elsa gazed at him, round-eyed.

"How did you know who I be."

"Well," he answered stolidly, "I be a kind of cousin of your father's.   Ye bear too much resemblance to Elsbet for me to mistake ye."

Elsa's fear gave way to a great wave of comforting relief.   Here was someone who knew her, who was not unfriendly.   She told them of her mother, and the witch hunter, and the storm.

Melchior gazed at her with great, mournful black eyes, and now and again he crossed himself.   Werner looked at Hans and Hans gazed at Werner, but when Elsa had finished her story and had fallen into a sorrowful silence they said nothing.   The girl stared at them a moment, then seeing their hesitation she rose.

"I thank you, good sirs, for taking care of me.   I must go back to Lutz and find my Fräulein Bach, for she is all that is left to me now.   If they catch me, I care not."   She curtsied respectfully to each musician, and walked slowly, for she felt very tired and forlorn again, down the green path which led toward

the highway. Small animals scurried from her footsteps as she went, but none were so lonely as she. They
were like her neighbors, and all of those she had known
in Lutz; they fled from her as though she had a foul
disease. Elsa looked at the pathway through a film of
tears, and wondered where she could go, what she could
do, alone.

She jumped nervously. There was a shout behind
her. Werner bounced into sight waving a wriggling,
squirming black object in his fat hands.

"Fräulein, here is your cat, which I did find upon
your skirt last night and did put in my pouch, leaving
it in the bushes so its cries would not wake you. I clean
forgot it. And a thousand plagues upon it, for it
scratched me right smartly when I took it out."

Elsa stumbled to the Fräulein, and took her into her
arms with a sob of gratitude.

"Ah, thank you, for now I need not look for my
Fräulein. I can take the road to Nürnberg, as my
mother bade me."

"Fräulein! That is your Fräulein? We thought
ye spoke of some friend in Lutz." And he led her
back to their fire.

"Hans," cried Werner, "the maid has no friends
here. She is a wanderer now, even as we are. She
must make her way, alone, she says, to Nürnberg."

Hans stared at the girl, so small and slight in her
faded blue cloak.

"Nürnberg is a goodly city, with much regard for
musicians," he said slowly.

"Yea," cried Werner, "an well do the Nürnbergers pay for their pleasures.   'Twould be a profitable place to head for."

"Nay," the deep voice of Melchior startled them, "with a black katze I will not go.   It be the instrument of the Devil.   I will have nought to do with it. With the little maid, but not with her katze."   He crossed himself.   Werner and Hans bade the girl sit down, then they took their friend to one side.   Elsa heard the voice of Hans rumbling, and saw the arms of Werner waving, but Melchior only shook his head back and forth, pendulum-wise.

"I must look after her," said Hans.

"Nay, I go not with a witch," spoke Melchior.

"But," shouted Werner, "she cannot be a witch, for Hans knows herself and her mother.   And think you can let a small maid go the long road to Nürnberg alone?   She would get no farther than the highway.   She is the kinsmaid of Hans.   We must go with her.   What matters to us which direction?"

"Nay, I go not with a witch and a black cat."

"Then will we two part from you," roared Werner.

Elsa jumped up nervously.   "Nay, good Werner," she called, "ye shall not break your friendship for me. I will go alone."   She grasped the kitten more closely, and walked again, quickly, down the path.   She was so small, so panic-stricken under the big trees, but she only smoothed the soft fur of her friend and walked as fast as she could.   Her throat felt choked.

What was that? She heard a noise ahead of her. There came the sound of leaves protesting against some moving object which trampled down the growth at the sides of the narrow path. Elsa stopped, shaking. Could it be that smeller-out of witches? Another rustle of leaves from behind! She looked around and saw Hans and Werner hurrying to her. They paused suddenly to listen. Then, grasping her unceremoniously, Hans swung her up and ran back to their resting place. He thrust her behind a dense clump of bushes, and sat down again, indifferently, on the grass. Werner did likewise, and Melchior stretched out on the other edge of the undergrowth, pretending sleep.

Gentle snoring from the lank fellow accompanied the loud conversation suddenly begun by Werner and Hans. Elsa peeped fearfuly through the leaves, and held her kitten with rigid arms. The muscle in the back of her neck felt like a stretched cord. She saw the path filled with a big body, and a small sighing breath of relief escaped her lips as she gazed at a soldier in a buff jerkin, who carried a cross-bow, and who stared with a hairy, suspicious face around the little glade.

"What wouldst, friend?" called Werner cordially. "We have no food to offer, being poor wandering musicians, but we can give an honest bowman a seat upon good turf and a pleasant morsel of chatter."

The soldier advanced a few paces and spoke in a hoarse voice, "Hast seen aught of a small maid and the

Devil's instrument, a black cat, with which she works her evil deeds on good men?"

"Nay," answered Werner easily, "an did we see such a person we would run in three directions, for by the wild beast demons of St. Anthony I like not witches myself. But why so excited, friend?"

"Zounds! And reason enough! By her foul means of sorcery she fled from the convent of St. Clare where my master had found her to be, after she escaped in the crowd from Lutz. An now a peasant living near the cloister proclaims that he saw her sail from the place on a broomstick at midnight, with lighted sulphurous vapors around her and the black cat a-sitting on her devilish yellow head. But if ye have not seen her I must needs look further."

He turned in his steps. There was a small squeal of rage from the tightly clutched Fräulein, and with a leap she left Elsa's arms and bounded into the astounded gaze of the soldier. He crossed himself hurriedly, glaring fiercely at Werner.

His red whiskers bristled angrily. Avoiding Fräulein Bach, who was unconcernedly chasing a blowing leaf, he strode to the thicket and drew forth the trembling girl.

"Vixen," he cried, "charm me not, for ye cannot work evil with the Rohte Hahn. I like not the thought of taking ye, but needs must risk your spells." Facing Werner angrily, "And you . . . you will go too, for you lied for a witch."

Hans gazed longingly at his heavy oaken staff, across the glade, and therefore useless to him. The soldier stood between the two men and their weapons. Werner raged at the bowman, who only held Elsa the tighter, and turned to go, but with a wary eye cocked at the men in front of him. He motioned them to march before. Hans looked about for Melchior, who had disappeared as if the earth had swallowed him. There was but a long depression in the grass where he had lain. They entered the path, with the bowman belligerently following, his weapon in hand. Elsa clutched her kitten, and stared in front of her, with a pale face.

But as they walked they heard a faint rustling among the bushes bordering the narrow path. There was a sudden bellow from the soldier, and a cry from Werner. Elsa screamed. She saw a pair of huge bony hands thrust from the underbrush and grasp the legs of the Red Cock, who tumbled headlong, sending her and her two friends down with him. There was a mad scramble, terrifying to Elsa, who pulled herself to one side. It looked as if beggars were fighting for coins on a feast day. Four pairs of legs waved wildly, four throats shouted curses, and four heads cracked, one after the other, as fists, hard as iron, smote them. Elsa covered her face and trembled, until the noise died down to a rumble of satisfaction from Hans mixed with raging remarks from the bowman. She found the courage to look up. Her three new friends had the fellow fast, on the ground among torn

branches and leaves. There was a trickle of blood
on his head.

"Ah, Melchior," shouted Werner, wiping a bloody
nose, "ye have saved the maid!"

"Yea," spoke the lean man, "and why I know not,
for I do be afeard of witches."

"A plague on him!" roared the soldier. "Who
would think such a bag of sleeping bones could seize
upon me from behind?" He lapsed into sullen silence. Elsa lay on the ground where she had fallen
in the struggle, and hid her pale face in her arms. She
looked up at last, still trembling, to see her friends
binding the soldier securely with strips from Werner's cloak, which could spare some cloth and still be
too big for the little man. They took from the fellow
his weapons and tossed him in a thicket.

"Methinks 'twill cool the ire of Sir Rosy Crown to
sleep here a bit," remarked Werner; "and when he is
found by his friends he will have had time to concoct a
right marvelous tale of how all five of us, including the
lively Fräulein, cut the comb of this bold Red Cock,
and then flew away in a brimstone cloud a-riding on
his cross-bow."

Beyond the discomforted soldier's hearing they sat
them down to council. Elsa ceased to tremble, and,
with a timid look at the silent Melchior, came and sat
with them. It would not do at all to enter a town
near-by, or even a village, where the maid who had
fled could be recognized. Their problem was one of
food, for they had but a small amount of bread and

cheese with them, and very little money to buy more, even should they go to a town. Hans and Werner completely ignored Melchior's fear of Elsa, but the girl sent a small glance his way wonderingly. He was impassive, as usual, and looked half asleep.

The thing to be done, they decided, was to get away as quickly as possible, leaving one of them in the baron's forest to poach a deer. The hunter must be he who could best shoot an arrow. Werner was eliminated at once, for he knew not the art.

Spoke Werner: "Melchior, namesake of the Wise Man, canst bend a bow?"

"Yea," answered the lank one solemnly and very, very sadly. "Yea, but not so well. And I like not the thought of crashing madly through forest, bow in hand, to send an arrow into the flank of a deer. 'Tis passing hard on a fellow who has difficulty in carrying his dudelsack." And the long man sighed prodigiously.

"Whether you know the art well matters not, for yours be the lengthy arm for the work. So get you up and at it. We will divide the bread and cheese equally between all of us, then get us to the village which lies just on the other side of the forest. We must go slowly for the sake of the maid. And we will await you there at the edge of the wood, near the highway to the village. Hans will go further for bread while we wait. So be not too long at it, and bag a fine fat piece of meat."

The bit of food was divided among the four. Elsa

placed hers in the small bag at her belt.   She smoothed
the Fräulein as she did so, and secretly slipped her a
crumb of cheese.

"Fräulein," she whispered, "this is from my share,
so cannot injure our new friends.   But mayhap they
might prevent me from giving you some, for we have
very little.   But you need it as much as I.   Ah, Fräulein, we are indeed alone in the world, but not so alone
as we were last evening.   These be rough fellows, but
I fear them not—save the lean one."

She felt a slight movement behind her, and saw on
the edge of her cloak another portion of bread and
cheese.   Looking up in astonishment she glimpsed
Melchior crossing himself as he crashed his way into
the depth of the forest, cross-bow trailing from his
bony hand.

Werner picked up his cither, slung it about his neck,
and grasped his staff.   Elsa tried to fit her short step
to Hans' stride, and the Fräulein ran before and behind and sometimes between their feet, making frequent excursions up trees and down again along the
path.   A late morning sun was stripping the forest
of its chill.   Birds fussed shrilly at the kitten.   Life
could never be so carefree as it had been just two
long days ago, but the girl's spirits rose from a
trough of misery on the succeeding wave of adventure,
induced by a thousand scents and sights of the
wood.

After a while Werner threw his staff under one arm,
and took hold of the neck of his bowl-shaped instru-

ment, picking on the strings. And as he went he sang lustily, and this was the burden of his song!

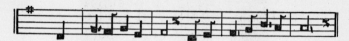

"A wanderer I be on a road that's wild and free.
Oh, a restless blade I be, an the end I cannot see.

An if ye prate of a vagabond's fate, what matters that to me?
My home's the spot where I am not, the rough road calls to me."

Chapter IV

TAKE WHAT SEEMS GOOD

AT the edge of the forest Elsa fell on the grass, her muscles crying for rest, even though the strong arms of big Hans had carried her part of the way. She turned an uninterested ear to the discussion between her two friends as to the best means of getting bread. She was too tired to be hungry, and, wrapped in her cloak, she fell asleep immediately, with the Fräulein curled up beside her. The last thing she saw as dusk fell upon them was a huge fire flaming to the sky, and Hans preparing to take up the first watch, a precaution which the wolves of the forest made necessary.

Next morning, with bread and cheese gone, all appetites compelled first attention.

"I'll go with my cither and sing to the village churls," spoke Werner.

"Nay," said Hans, "know ye not that these folk will hardly pause to listen an it is not a feast day. Ye

could make never a stiver so early in the morning.
I'll go."

"Your music will draw no more than mine."

"That I know, but I have a stouter arm to be hired.
Expect me not till sundown."

"Then," answered Werner, nodding to Elsa, "I'll
stay with the maid and make for her a pair of thick
sandals to wear over those thin shoes. But, methinks
you will fail also in the village. Ah, if you bring
bread, then perhaps Melchior will appear with meat
and so might we have a feast here in the edge of the
wood."

"That will I then," said Hans.

Werner drew a pair of worn-out boots from his
big bag and began to cut and curve the better parts
of the soles. "Once," he remarked to the girl, "I was
a passing fine cobbler, and not so long agone, neither."

Hans plodded stolidly to the houses, where women
were collected around neighborhood wells, with
turned-up skirts above gay ruffles, filling jugs with
water for the morning's work and at the same time
stuffing their ears with gossip. They stared at him
curiously. Hans strode on through the crooked
streets, almost disjointing his neck at times trying to
avoid stepping on children and pigs and poultry.
From small windows good hausfraus shook plump
feather covers; maid servants with bare red arms
smiled at the big fellow. Hans noticed none of them,
but made for the nearest large inn, which, he thought,
must surely be on the market place.

Reaching a large building of two stories Hans gazed about for the sign, but could see none. A moral inscription was painted in gilt letters across the front, and above the central door swung an iron lantern.

"This must be a tavern," thought the musician, so he pounded mightily on the oaken boards.

There was no response.

He thumped again, and with a huge hand shook the door.

Still no answer.

He drummed both fists with a noise like thunder.

A small upper window flew open to emit a frowsy head with a red nose and a pair of little angry eyes.

"Get ye to the rear door; this one opens not save it be later in the day." The head disappeared.

Hans, muttering explosively, plodded around to the back, where he found a tiny door so small that he was obliged to stoop to enter. As he came into a big kitchen, furnished on one side with numerous pots and a small table and bench, and on the other with an immense earthen stove, he perceived the man stumping in from the dark depths of the building.

"What would ye, at this early hour?" grumbled the fellow.

Hans bowed low.

"Worthy sir, I would have a place with you as baker, pot-boy, cook, waiter or chambermaid."

"Humph! Ye look strong enough." The man stared at him. "My stable man has gone this week since, and I do need help, but ye must do the stable

work and wait on customers inside too.   I'll pay ye
five batzen and your victuals."

"'Tis passing little wage for a full grown man.   But
when the belly cries for food we needs must hearken."

The inn-keeper pointed beyond the yard sourly and
bade his new yokel go clean the pig pen, for it had not
been touched since before the departure of the former
servant.

"Nay," said Hans, who smelled fresh bread a-baking
in the oven, "do all that hard work I cannot till my
appetite be answered.   I must have food."

"A plague on ye and your appetite," grumbled the
man, but he waddled about till he found an infinitesimal
loaf, so small on its big trencher that it resembled a
lone rock on a vast expanse of wooden desert.   This
and a jug of watery wine he set down before Hans,
who was seated on the bench.   With a grin the inn-
keeper remarked, waving his hand, "Take what seems
good to you."

Hans stared at it ruefully, but only answered,
"That will I then," and set to.   The fellow disappeared again into the recesses of his house.   It took
but a moment for the musician to polish off every
crumb and drain the jug dry.   As he sat there in-
wardly rumbling curses on the stingy host he heard
a scratching on the earth floor and saw a fat hen which
had just wandered in through the open door and was
trying busily to dig some sustenance from the hard-
packed ground.   A tiny but energetic thought buzzed
into the head of Hans and settled there comfortably.

He reached for the unlucky hen and with one swift twist her neck was off. He placed her neatly in his leather pouch and grinned. There was a small noise at the outer door. Again a chicken walked importantly in. Again it met its fate, but not without some frantic squawking. A third bird followed her unfortunate sisters, and this time the noise was so earsplitting that, just as Hans placed her in his bulging bag, the inn-keeper, crimson with rage, ran into the kitchen.

"What is this, you thief? Taking my good fowls! I'll have the soldiers on ye!"

Hans looked stupidly at him, blue gaze impassive.

"Master," he said solemnly, "you bade me take what seemed good to me, and that I did, for never have I put eye on fowls which seemed better."

The inn-keeper quivered with rage and his red nose grew purple.

"Well sir, an ye take these fowls ye work for me till the New Year, and never one stiver do ye get for it. Ye will pay me in good hard labor for this."

Hans bowed without a smile, and nodded agreeably.

"Master, I am your servant," he said.

"Then get ye to that sty. Take out the swine and clean the place."

Hans went, and when he reached the place he felt some sympathy for the animals who had to live there, for they were of a certainty penned in filth. "This job," he thought, "would indeed take till the New Year."

A greasy hog, with a reddish thick nose and a pair of small mean eyes stared at him disagreeably.

"Methinks," said the new hand, "ye do resemble your kinsman in the inn. Now he told me to take ye out, but said not where to put ye. Mayhap ye would feel at ease in his company. If that inn is good enough for him, 'tis good enough for ye."

With some difficulty he managed to haul and shove his squealing charges to the kitchen door and inside. He closed the door and then went back to the sty, and was just getting ready to enter its filth when a terrible uproar burst upon his ear.

"What a din! What a din! How can a man work in such a clatter?"

The noise grew louder. There was a strange mixture of squawks and squeals and shrieks, until Hans gave up work in disgust and plodded to the kitchen door. There was a fragrant odor of freshly baked bread, which cooled pleasantly upon the table. But the floor was a whirling, grunting, squeaking mass of swine and hens. One obese sow emitted agonizing noises as she was pursued about by a stout enraged woman with brawny arms and a kerchief on her head. The woman uttered shrieks, which rose above pig and hen sounds, and all moved round and round as if on a treadmill.

The inn-keeper burst through the house door. A mad porker ran between his fat legs, rolling him over and over. Hans leaned against the outside doorpost

and surveyed the wild scene in astonishment and some disapproval.

"Zut! Zut!" rumbled Hans reprovingly to the fat man.

The inn-host regained his feet, and on that instant he heard Hans.   He shook his fist frenziedly.

"Churl! Vagabond! What made ye let these beasts loose in my tavern?"

"Where else was there to put them?   Ye bade me take out the swine and clean the sty, and that did I do, but for the plaguey noise which disturbed me at my labors."

The man sputtered and spit.

"Hadn't ye sense enough to tie them outside?   Why stand ye there and not help catch these animals?"

"Ye did not tell me to catch beasts, but only to take them out.   I came in here because my nose caught a whiff of the fine cookery."

"May the Foul Fiend take ye!   Get ye from my house!"

"Nay," said Hans, "ye bade me serve here, and here I serve."   He plunged into the room and pursued the pigs furiously, sending them into wilder and wilder confusion, until the inn-keeper was beside himself. He jumped and squealed and squawked as loud as any animal.   "Methinks his resemblance to his beasts grows more striking every minute," thought Hans.

The host wheeled about and saw nothing within reach to vent his rage on but rows of fresh bread cooling on the table.   Seizing a big loaf he threw it at the head of Hans, who was lustily chasing a slippery little pig among the pots.   Hans gasped from the impact, then picked up the loaf, leaped to the door, bowed low his thanks, and departed with all speed; the noise of struggle and the yells of his employer pursued him as he went.

Hans concealed his booty as he approached the edge of the wood.   What was that sound?   Borne on a gentle breeze was a rollicking tune, startling the meadow mice around him.

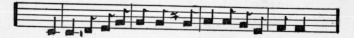

"The noble wears fine closen, the soldier dons gay hosen,"

The maid decks out in rosen, red shoes the burgher goes in,"

"Methinks have I heard that voice before," murmured Hans.

"An churls have feathers chosen to ape the wealthy breed.

An we have but our nosen to follow where they lead."

"Hah!" spoke Hans, "Werner sings.   Melchior must be here."   The big fellow smacked his lips in anticipation of venison steak.

He entered their camp and saw Melchior stretched out upon the grass.   Elsa was busily engaged with a needle and thread from Werner's overflowing pouch, and Werner sat, hand on cither, singing with gusto.

"Hola, Hans!" shouted the little man, leaping up. "Come, tell us your luck? Melchior has this instant returned, but will do nought but snore."

Hans turned to Elsa,

"Why," he rumbled, "she has mended Werner's cloak where we drew the strips to bind yon red head. And 'tis neat as noodles. Maid, I foresee we shall be vagabonds no longer but shall soon go decent as towns-folk on way to Easter mass." He smiled down at her, and Elsa blushed.

"You do so much for me. And this is little in re-turn. If you, good Hans, will give me your cap I can mend in a trice the disorderly rent in it."

Hans handed over his headgear and faced Melchior.

"Ho, namesake of the Wise Man, where is the meat?"

Melchior sat up slowly, and his eyes were very sad. Elsa's face turned sorrowful in sympathy. She felt almost tearful as she looked at him. Melchior sighed deeply, and said in a mournful voice,

"Alack! I did have a long day after ye all left me there in forest with a quiver of arrows and no sight nor sound of meat. I walked till my legs did give beneath me, and not for hours did I see the dun coat of deer. Then one ran out. I fitted an arrow. I let fly. The animal bounded into the leaves, and may I grow as fat as Werner here if that creature did not turn and slowly lower one eyelid offensively at me. The bolt was trembling in a tree trunk."

Melchior sighed again profoundly. Elsa's sympathetic distress gave way to a smile as she saw Werner break into a broad grin.

"And did Sir Deer call ye a dunderdolt into the bargain?" he asked.

Melchior gave him a reproachful look.

"Deeper into the wood I went on protesting shanks, and many arrows did I send after that deer, but never once could I hit the mark. Methought the Fowl Fellow of the Cloven Hoof himself inhabited those pesky animals. And so soon as that entered my mind I bethought me we would not want to eat meat of the Devil, so I lay out to sleep a bit. My joints did yearn for rest."

"'Twas an exceeding convenient decision, and one which liked you well, I doubt not," commented Werner dryly.

"I was just closing my eyes," continued the lean one, ignoring the interruption, "when a flash of brown drew me up and at it, groaning mightily. I fitted an arrow to my bow cunningly. The deer looked at me a minute, then darted into a thinly defined path. I bounded after, fleet as the deer."

Werner roared suddenly at the vision of the bony frame of Melchior leaping fleetly as a deer. Melchior refused to notice him.

"I let fly a bolt just as he disappeared. Missed again! No, I saw a tiny patch of buff among the leaves, close to the ground. I sent an arrow whizzing to it. And then, if all the spirits in the lower regions did not wail in one horrid voice!   There was a mighty din, but the noise sounded passing human for an animal.   I advanced cautiously and saw that same bowman, the great Rohte Hahn, pinned to earth with his own arrow through his jerkin.   There was a slight trickle of blood on his sleeve, and seeing it, the bumpkin groaned as though his very life were ebbing away."

Elsa gasped, but Werner bounded up and capered about in glee, laughing uproariously,

"Didst kill the fellow, Melchior?"

"Nay," said the lank one, "I but drew the arrow out, and found it had done little harm.   'What,' moaned the bowman, 'would ye return to slay me with my own bolts?   Do but kill me at once and cease this inhuman slaughter by piecemeal.   Ah-hh-hh!   Alack for the day I set out to take a witch maid, for this do be the result of her evil charms!' "

" 'Ye plaguey rogue,' I told him, 'why should I want to harm ye?   I did but shoot at a deer, and hit a coward instead.   It is a circle I have wandered in.   Hold your noise, before I put another arrow in your churlish carcass!   I'd as lief put these into your body head end first,' I said, laying down his arrows beyond his reach; and then I set off to find you.   But night caught me at it, and I had to spend the dark hours in a treetop, listening to wolves tearing the trunk to bits below me."

"The wolves would have had a sorry meal off your bones," commented Werner.

"Ne'er did I beg a game like that before," said the

long man, "an marry, I think he would make a passing tough meat roasted on a spit."

Elsa smiled at Melchior, "I am glad ye did not hurt him grievously."

But Werner looked disappointed, his dreams of venison steak sadly shattered. "And that be all ye got?" he muttered.

He drew his cither to him. "Welladay!" he cried, "if I cannot eat, I can sing."

Elsa felt a yearning emptiness within her at the prospect of another fasting day, but she said nothing.

"Come," rumbled Hans, after a silence, "we must go from here, for I glimpsed a dark man, in black, enter that village as I left it.

Elsa jumped up convulsively. "Ah, Hans, then we must away, and hasten, for that may be the witch-smeller-out, who is himself the Evil One."

"Nay," spoke Melchior, "I have used my legs too much of late. He will not discover us here."

"Then I go without you all." Elsa grasped her sleeping kitten in her arms, threw her cloak about her and ran through the fields, stumbling over clods of earth, but dashing on in a frenzy. Hans was soon beside her.

"We are coming too, maid, and by night we will be far from here. Go not without us!"

She was gasping for breath, sobbing jerkily, but the presence of Hans beside her was comforting. She could hear Werner puffing along in the rear and Melchior grumbling behind her.

"These learned doctors are the Devil's minions," cried Werner when they all walked together again, "They are everywhere at once, like the plaguey fleas of Italy."

When they had left the sight of village smoke behind, and there was no noise of pursuit, Elsa breathed easier, and they sat down to rest. She was faint with hunger and fatigue, and her companions looked as if a great slice of venison still lingered in their thoughts. Hans began to build a fire.

"What are doing?" cried Werner irritably. "'Tis not so cold that we need a blaze by day. Wolves come but in the dark. And there's nought to roast over it but our shins."

"What callest this?" answered Hans, drawing from his pouch the hens, and producing the loaf from under his jacket.

Elsa looked up at the fat man's shout. It was a miracle. There had been nothing; now there was food. How it got there did not seem to matter. She did not even ask.

"Aha!" grinned Werner slyly, after a while, as he threw the last scrap to Fräulein Bach, "the maid becomes a vagabond. It concerns her not how she lives, but only that she lives. The wind on a road gives zest to one's palate."

"And danger to one's neck," muttered Hans.

CHAPTER V

ACH! FRÄULEIN BACH!

THE road was long, and often hard for small plodding feet, unused to vagabond ways. Elsa felt that her strength was taxed to its utmost capacity; sometimes her head reeled with utter weariness. But she knew that she could stand everything that came, if it were only possible to keep her face and hands clean. Somehow she was uncomfortable when dirty, for never before had she had intimate association with the earth. At each brook she insisted on stopping to wash, while Melchior crossed himself apprehensively, fearing the dabblings of witchcraft; the other two comrades watched her in silent amazement. At first they were impatient, but soon learned that this, for some strange reason, was necessary to the maid. Before long Elsa saw, with amusement, that the three furtively washed their hands and faces as she did, and she whispered to the kitten, "Fräulein, it do be a big improvement, too."

One day the wanderers drew near a queer crowd of tattered travelers, whose men walked with a swagger in spite of their filthy, gaudy rags, and whose women, hard-faced, swung short skirts above bare brown ankles, as wailing, fighting children clung to them. There were goats and hens and dogs following along, making the countryside hideous with noise. Elsa shrank from them, but Werner joined the one-eyed cutthroat who led the party. He returned full of glee, telling his friends that the gypsies were on their way to a fine wedding in the castle of Swartzenstein near-by, where there would be enough meat and drink for all.

"This knight of the Schloss Swartzenstein," remarked Werner, "they do say lives like a prince himself, an't please you, and gives with a right liberal hand. He is not one of the princes, member of the emperor's court, but is a knight, with his own estate, peasants and courtly household. He is betrothed to the Lady Katherina, of high rank, who comes to him on the morrow for the wedding ceremony. They do say the noble is drunk with joy, and mayhap with Rhenish wine also, for the fair dame brings with her a stupendous dowry. Heaven grant this lord be not like many another knight who both plows and takes purses on a weekday, then piously enters chapel on a Sunday dressed in a scarlet mantle."

Elsa listened with but one ear, for she could not

keep from her thoughts the burning eyes of the doctor, and the approach of a crowd made her nervous.

Presently Hans suggested that they rest and let the gypsies go on ahead, for his legs, he said, were about to give out. Melchior thought how strange it was that Hans of late had needed so much rest, but he ceased to wonder in thankfulness at having a chance to stretch out for a little sleep.

Elsa sat down gratefully. And as they rested there soon came up with them two beggars, one with his head done up in a dirty rag and the other with a lame knee, which caused him to limp badly. They were loaded with trinkets and shells, hung around hairy necks. Halting before the musicians they whined:

"Come, buy a sacred relic from the mount of Calvary. This bit of wood is a piece of the tree on which our Lord died."

But Hans irreverently shook his shaggy head at them, and Werner rose profanely to bid them begone, or by a long list of sacred objects he would thrust their relics down their throats. The beggars took to their heels, their valuable cargo jingling as they fled. Elsa noticed with astonishment that the fellow with his head bound up lost his rag and never saw it, and the man with the lame knee made off on both legs, dropping his infirmity as he went. And, as a matter of fact, he ran faster than his miserable companion.

"Alas!" cried she, "that the good Lord should allow such thieverly fellows to sell his precious relics."

"Maid," rumbled Hans, "do not believe all that

you see upon the road.   These men sell no precious relics, but worthless imitations to gull the innocent."

Werner grinned and picked up the Fräulein.

"Melchior," he said slyly, "your pouch be larger and emptier than either of ours.   'Tis there the lively Fräulein must ride."

"Nay, nay," pleaded the lank one, but he made no more protest when Werner installed the kitten within, leaving an air hole at the top.

The little party again rose and went upon its way toward the castle of Swartzenstein.   Passing through farm country they came to a hill overlooking a town, but did not enter there.   They waited outside while Hans went in to buy, with their few remaining pence, bread and cheese.   As they left the region Werner pointed to four frowning gray castles on bare rock outside the town and told Elsa how they were occupied by knights of noble lineage.

"In the oldest castle," he said, "lived Bligger von Steinach, who gave the name of Steinach to this town. He was a robber baron, and forsooth the most successful old rogue in these parts.   But his fate overtook him, as it has a goodly way of doing, and one morning he was found a-lying in his own blood in his own courtyard. The murderer could not be discovered, but natheless his son, believing the air a trifle too disagreeable for him there, left at once for the Holy Land with the Crusaders.

"It was in Palestine that he cut down the heathen right and left and hewed and hacked right valiantly on their carcasses. Wherefore he covered himself with glory along with heathen gore. Well, the story runs, that this brave fellow was so full of pious zeal that he could not rest till he had chopped off the head of the sultan himself. So the young baron, full of guile, disguised himself as a harper—he played passing well on that instrument—and strummed himself into the household of the monarch. There he seized the sultan while the trusting heathen slept, and secured his head, which he brought in triumph home. Once he was in Christian camp, the emperor knighted him and gave him the sultan's head as a crest. Thus was that noble house founded, in Christian zeal and knightly ardor."

"Well," said the girl, wrinkling her small forehead, "I like not the thought of a house founded on treachery."

"Wherefore blame a Christian for doing his duty?" answered Werner dryly. "Maid, if ye would romance about these noble families look not too closely into their origins."

Next day the crowd grew denser on the way to Swartzenstein. Suddenly around a bend in the road appeared the castle, a great rambling pile of stone set upon a hill above the peasant houses. The bridge across the old moat was covered with a moving stream of servants, jostling peasants and shouting retainers. And, just going into the castle grounds were the Bohemians, brilliant in their dirty finery. Everywhere was the intoxicating air of excitement, so that Elsa, for all her sad thoughts, felt it necessary to tell the Fräulein about the strange things she saw.

"And I wouldn't be surprised, Fräulein," she said, "if I could find ye a fat piece of beef there. But ye must not whimper, for we cannot take ye out in such a crowd. They would cry 'Satan' at ye."

Entering the castle gateway they plunged into a whirlpool of raucous confusion in the courtyard. Peddlers hawked their wares; the Bohemians had set up tattered tents and were telling the fortunes of gullible peasants, while babies screamed and musicians played and the din increased. Puffing men-servants dashed about like a stirred nest of ants getting in each other's way, shouting imperative orders which were never obeyed, and stumbling over everything. Barefoot maid-servants carried things thither and yon, and flirted with vagabonds and farmers indiscriminately, their cheeks red with excitement and their holiday skirts wide and brilliant in hue.

As the little group of musicians searched for a corner to settle in, they looked around eagerly at the furious uproar. Elsa stood in a daze, gazing and wondering. Her eye passed over the head of a tall, thin youth, with long wavy brown hair, and came to rest on his quiet face, alien to the noisy crowd. He was standing alone, isolated from confusion, and looked on with an amused and wistful expression. He wore a suit of nondescript cut, with ragged shoes, and around his neck was suspended a leather bag. Werner glanced at Elsa, then looked that way.

"Ah, may I bake on a gridiron, if 'tis not Conrad, who walked beside us and shared our bread last summer." The explosive little man bounced across, among the moving folk, and threw his arm around the shoulder of the surprised youth, who needed but a glance to reflect his pleasure. Conrad joined them, staring at Elsa in amazement, consumed with curiosity.

"An what brings you here, friend?" rumbled Hans, when they had told him the girl's story. The youth sighed.

"Ah, that I know not . . . exactly," he spoke hesitatingly. "But I thought I wanted to 'prentice myself to that goldsmith in Augsburg . . . then the life irked me. Bothered . . . worried me. I meant to stay . . . but I left."

"Welladay," commented Werner, lifting one eyebrow, "dost know what ye like ever?"

Conrad frowned.

"Yea, sometimes . . . but not for long." He looked down at the broken toe of his boot which he was moving in the dust, and seemed to study gravely the pattern made thereby. "Yea, but I thought the itch my fingers have . . . satisfied by being a goldsmith. But 'tis too mechanical . . . he would not let me make my own designs . . . too dull."

"If a goldsmith's life does not suit ye, then what do ye want to stop that finger itch?" said Werner quietly.

Conrad looked uncomfortable. Then he answered slowly as if scarcely able to frame his thoughts in words.

"I be restless, Werner . . . forever searching . . . wanting to make things . . . beautiful things . . . but not goldsmithry." He lifted his head suddenly, defiantly, as if he were afraid that he might be laughed at. "I think overmuch on this . . . but feel more than think. To draw and paint with fine colors . . . that's what I want."

Hans stared at Melchior in astonishment, and the long man gazed back at him blankly. They knew not what he meant. Elsa too stared, first at the embarrassed boy, then at the three musicians. She wondered. This must be something important, but it was very mysterious to her. Did he mean to paint those figures which hung in the churches? And why did he want to so much. All she understood was that he did want to . . . very much.

Werner did not stare. He smiled understandingly, this time without a raised eyebrow, and with none of his usual sly humor.

"Then, lad," he said softly, "canst do no better than come with us, for we turn our nosen toward Nürnberg, where every house front be painted, an they do say that even the main spouts are of fine copper gilded with gold and fashioned like flying dragons. I know not why ye should want to hold a brush, when ye might try to be a musician," he turned to Melchior, with a comic down-drawing of the corners of his mouth, "but I know not, neither, why this bag of bones plays the dudelsack, when he might find a soft corner and sleep the clock around instead. Why go ye

to Nürnberg, friend Melchior?"   Werner opened his
mouth very wide and laughed silently.

"Why, indeed?   I go only to get a view of those curious Nürnberg eggs, which, they say, do fit in a man's
clothes snugly, and tell the time of day.   I like not the
thought of taking a black cat, but I cannot forswear
the sight of a clock which a fellow might carry in
his palm."

Elsa felt hurt.   She turned to Melchior, ready to
take her Fräulein from his pouch.   Then the girl noticed how the long man shifted his bag carefully to give
the kitten more air and make her more comfortable.
Werner winked at Hans.

Food was easy to get, far easier than to talk in the
confusion.   Elsa stared, astonished, and listened and
looked wide-eyed.

"Make way!   Make way!   Make way for the
bride!" cried a tall chamberlain in crimson hose, with
parti-colored red and blue doublet, and a staff in his
hand.   He marched solemnly through the courtyard
and the retainers, stung to furious energy by this, re-
doubled their efforts and managed, by shoving bump-
kins out of the way, to make a lane from the bridge
to the castle door.   From the kitchen came a luscious
odor of roast venison and fresh puddings and many
other appetizing smells.   Elsa sniffed and wrinkled her
nose.   The Fräulein caught a whiff also, which proved
too much for her self-control, but her cries went un-
heard in the uproar, and nobody so much as turned a
head her way.

A sudden silence fell as the clatter of horses was heard on the heavy wood of the bridge. A troup of gayly caparisoned riders galloped into the courtyard, and dismounted before the door. They were followed by a white steed from which a lady, with a nose like a gable overhanging her receding chin, wearing a pearl embroidered gown and with a gold net upon her flowing hair, dismounted, followed by her maids. Then the gaping audience saw a tall old man ride into the courtyard. Immediately the nobles disappeared into the castle; Werner whispered to Elsa that the old man must be the lady's guardian or father.

"Ah," breathed Elsa, "if I could but see the wedding ceremony."

"'Tis but a ceremony," said Hans, "for, maid, you know that the betrothal is the real binding act; this trumpery wedding is but the handing over of bride and dowry to the bridegroom."

"But an the maid wishes to see it," spoke Melchior surprisingly, "I can hold her up above the crowd."

So the tall fellow took Elsa on his broad shoulder and thereby raised her eyes above the heads of a mob which filled the doorway. Inside there was a dazzling display of color in the gaudy clothes of both guests and retainers. As Elsa looked she saw the spindle-legged old man hand to the red-faced knight a straw, a ring, a stick and an arrow, which the noble received with a bow. These, explained Werner in a loud tone, which drew an angry frown from one of the guards, were articles given the bride by her near husband at

the betrothal ceremony to guarantee money to her
should she ever be a widow. They stood for a sum
in gold, and were in return for the dowry money,
given by the bride. It was, Werner remarked, rather
like the purchase of a heifer.

The conclusion of the ceremony was in progress under the banners of the noble families. The bridegroom
was giving to the bride a sword, a hat and a mantle,
signifying the protection he intended to accord to her
in future. A great blast of horns signaled the com-
pletion of the wedding. Elsa was lowered quickly
as the mob parted for the knight and his bride, who
came from the dim hall to the chapel across the yard
to have their union blessed.

Then confusion rolled in a wave across the throng.
Long tables set within the great hall groaned under
enormous bowls of broth, trenchers piled high with
goose and fowl and roast meats of every kind. Pigs
came in, roasted whole, and there was even a wild boar,
sizzling with fat. The wedding party gorged and
drank within the castle, while without food was passed
for peasants and poorer folk who had come to the
feast.

Elsa was a bit afraid to approach, so savage were
the men and women who ate there, some fighting
wolfishly over roast meat, tearing it to shreds. But
the musicians bade her take care of their precious instruments in the corner, and they found food to bring
to her. Conrad rushed back with a hen; Melchior

procured a horn of wine for her; Hans came in proudly with a pudding; Werner arrived with bread and cheese.

"Ah! good friends," gasped the girl, "never can I eat all of this fine food."

"What ye cannot eat stuff away in our pouches," spoke Werner, " for we gorge now, but we may starve to-morrow. And, Fräulein Bach," he admonished, "just hold your plaintive music till we can fill ye with good meat." Which, in truth, Elsa had already done before she had eaten her own share.

When the self-invited guests outside the hall were prone with too much eating the courtyard looked as if a thousand quivers of arrows, each shaft tipped with fat food, had laid them all low. The three musicians got their instruments, cither, dudelsack, and zinck, to coax from them a folk dance, popular in that vicinity.

As they played lustily they suddenly perceived a pompous chamberlain in feathers and ribbons and velvet finery standing before them. The music was quenched instantly. Elsa grew frightened, and pushed the Fräulein back in her bag.

"Goodmen," quoth the fellow, throatily, "my noble master has heard your piping, as has also his lady, and they bade me to have you all in to perform for them."

The musicians trailed after the chamberlain, and Conrad followed with Elsa, who felt small and untidy in her faded and soiled farthingale. She edged close to Melchior, who had her Fräulein tight in his bag; she had a wild desire to flee out the gate.

Inside rush lights burned in the hands of serving men. At the head of the largest table sat the knight, slumped over with wine, beside him was his wife. She held her hands over a bowl which a kneeling attendant held, while another poured rose water upon their fingers to wash away the grease and dough of their feast. At the noble's feet slept a great lean dog.

"Humph!" whispered Werner, "that dudish chamberlain lied when he said his master heard our music. He could not hear the veriest clap of thunder."

On the right hand of the host sat, in the splendor of rich vestments, the high dignitary of the church who had given his sanction to the wedding.

Elsa trembled anew when, at the conclusion of the music, she heard herself called by the lady.

"And has the maid no part in your performance that you leave her so silent?"

All eyes turned to the girl, who stood rooted to the floor, her cheeks stained red with embarrassment.

"Yea, my lady," spoke up Werner, bowing so profoundly that his cloak billowed out about him, "she but waited for an invitation. The maid sings like a nightingale."

"Then will she sing for me?"

Elsa looked at Werner, who pushed her forward and whispered to her to let them hear one of the songs he had taught her. He would accompany her on the cither. Hans moved close behind her.

Elsa screwed up her courage and sang. Her voice lingered, small and plaintive, in the rafters of the great hall. The lady bowed her head and handed Elsa a silver coin. The girl was murmuring her thanks, when there was a sudden rustling movement in the crowd about the doorway. A great fellow, in a buff jerkin, and with gingery whiskers covering a fierce countenance burst into the room and advanced until he stood almost behind the sodden knight's chair. Elsa glanced up and uttered a low cry.

Hans picked up the girl as if she were a piece of fluff borne by the wind. He made for the door roughly, crying to his comrades as he fled.

"Be off! Be off! The Red Cock!"

The crowd was too astonished to perceive what had happened. As the three friends followed close behind Hans, already dashing across the bridge, they heard a voice cry loudly, brazen as a gong.

"The witch maid! Seize her! The witch maid!"

There was an instant uproar. Soldiers stumbled madly about; the lackeys fell over each other. Peasants dropped on their knees, crossing themselves in a frenzy, and the one-eyed gypsy led his followers to their victims, where they began to pick folks pouches and cut their purses, unnoticed in the din.

But Hans was well on his way toward the near-by wood, and his comrades were not far behind. Elsa gasped and sobbed as she clung to her protector. She felt the hot short breath of Hans on her face, and saw the curly beard jerking with the violence of his ef-

fort.   Feet pounded on the bridge behind.   The pur-
suers were gaining.   Elsa's very sandals shook as she
heard the shouting and shrieking.   There was a throb-
bing in her ears, like the surf's impact against its
enemy the rock.   She flung an agonized glance over
Hans' shoulder and saw Werner's fat face, crimson,
and his short legs scudding along behind the longer
stride of Melchior and Conrad.   There were no pur-
suers in sight, and, at last, only a dull mumble of
sounds, of which the loudest was the wolf-like barking of some deep-throated dog.

As they entered the cool forest Hans stopped to take
breath, and wait for his companions, and then they
ran again, all together, deeper into the wood.

But as they fled, gasping from lungs ready to burst,
the Fräulein grew more and more frightened, and she
heard no answer to her anxious cries.   There was a
small opening in her abode, which she managed by
dint of frantic clawing to widen to a size that per-
mitted her small black head to emerge.   What she saw
froze her with horror.

Behind the running friends, who did not dare stop
to look back, was the big dog, his hot red tongue hanging.   Eyes mad with blood lust sent a needle of terror
through every erect hair on the cat's body.

"Alack," gasped Werner, "I can run no farther—my
breath do be leaving my body entirely!   And I hear
not the yells any longer.   They must have given us up
as lost."

The four stopped and dropped with one motion.
Elsa sat there listening with every nerve.   The cries

had ceased, but there was a thudding and panting coming nearer. And Elsa saw that her Fräulein had leaped from Melchior's pouch to the grass, where she stood stiffly, eyes sharpened to tiny points of green light.

Conrad paled at the sound, then jumped before Elsa with staff upraised.

"Oh, catch her!" gasped the girl, helpless with fear, but the men had no time to move a spent muscle. The big dog, teeth extended, ran into their opening between trees, with a growl full of menace. The Fräulein backed and backed until she reached a bowlder, and there she stood, petrified. The dog crouched for a spring at Melchior, who was nearest him, but before he could leap he saw the little cat against her stone. The eyes of the animal gleamed. He hurtled toward her. Elsa screamed shrilly and threw her arm across her eyes.

There was a loud hiss and then a terrible howl of pain. With one lightning stroke of tearing claws Fräulein Bach had ripped across the sensitive nose of the dog. He ran, yelping madly, toward the castle. Fräulein Bach stood rigid for a moment, then sat herself down and began washing her face as if she had never had more serious thoughts in all the days of her life.

"Look up, maid," shouted Werner, "for by all the Holy Saints in Christendom your Fräulein has routed the great dog!" Elsa held her arm tightly across her eyes, afraid to look, then she sprang across the grass and grasped her cat with a sob.

Melchior looked with grudging gratitude at the cat.

"Your katze has done us good service this time, maid," he said, "which cancels, by mathematics, with the time she brought the hulking soldier upon us."

"We are truly grateful, Fräulein Bach," said Werner, bowing low to the kitten, who purred contentedly in Elsa's arms. "Your bravery is only comparable to your sweet voice when you sing."

And so the wanderers turned their faces toward Nürnberg, hearing no more the din of a witch hunt, but thinking it best to travel as far as might be as soon as might be from that castle. And as they went Werner lifted his voice in song, bowing ever and anon to the Fräulein.

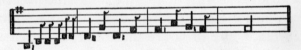

"Ach! Fräulein Bach! Fräulein Bach!
Think you the bride liketh her lot
Yoked to the knight who drinks like a sot?
Think you the knight liketh better his pot
Than to look at the bride when chin she hath not?
Think you the chamberlain giveth one jot
For handsomer legs than those he's got?"

Conrad laughed.

"Think you the churl goeth home to his cot
With broken bones and a pate that's hot?
Think you the Cock would see us shot
And brought in feet first to this very spot?
Think you the dog likes your claws, Gott Wott?
Ach! Fräulein Bach! Fräulein Bach!"

Chapter VI

WHERE ROADS END

Days on the road lengthened into weeks, until Elsa grew to love the wind in her face as she trudged along. She no longer got so weary, but could walk without much rest. Her dress and mantle grew ragged and soiled, though she stopped as often as she could to wash them; her sandals became paper thin. But Elsa's cheeks were brown, her eyes bright, and the sun brought color to her lips.

Then came St. Andrew's Day, the last of November, and the day when winter drew in to send good folk shivering to their warm tile stoves.

"Ss-ss-seven jackets and twelve pairs of h-h-hosen would not be enough to keep this wind from freezing our very marrow bones," chattered Werner, drawing his cloak tightly about him. "This vagabond life wears not well in a wintry breeze."

But the wanderers warmed themselves with the

thought of Nürnberg. Many times Conrad had told Elsa of the glories of Nürnberg, jewel of their Germany, where trade and art, music and artisanship met and mingled. Elsa looked with longing eyes toward the city, thinking of her kinsman. Werner spoke of the great Meistersingers there, and of how they had formed a guild to foster the composing of songs.

On this chilly day they had risen with good hearts, for, if they walked well, they should see the spires of Nürnberg by dusk. An hour on the way brought them up behind a lumbering cart, which was filled with rolls of hides, and which was driven by a gay young fellow in the hose and blouse of an artisan.

"Ho, there!" shouted Werner, as they approached within hailing distance, "can you give five wayfarers a ride into city? The maid here is growing weary."

The straw-haired man turned with a steady stare, and then, grinning at them pleasantly, bade the five climb in on the hides. Elsa, as Hans lifted her high on top of a roll, thought, with small puckered nose, that the smell was scarcely agreeable, but long before this she had learned to keep such thoughts to herself. The strong scent of cowhide was better than to feel the cold wind freeze her marrow. She burrowed deeper into the rolls of skins.

Werner climbed up beside the driver, and the other three accompanied Elsa on the hides.

"And what sort of a man may ye be?" asked the driver.

"A passing fine musician," said Werner.

"Musician!   I doubt me ye know the first principle of a song.   Come, give us one.   I sing, myself."

"You sing!   Why, you look as if the only song you could make would be sound of a cow bellowing for her calf."

"Zounds!   We shall try each other out."

Werner roared out a verse, and when he had finished his new friend startled the travelers with another. And so, to the sound of loud music they arrived at the gate of Nürnberg.   Elsa raised her head.

Beyond the stone walls was a glimpse of peaked roofs and shining spires, and still farther she could see the frowning castle on its rock with round tower and jutting abutments.   The girl stared, entranced.   In all her travels she had never before seen a big city.   Surely behind these massive stone walls her flight was ended. Surely the dark man and his fighting cock could never find her here.   This was the jolliest, the busiest, the friendliest of cities, or so they had told her.   The bright houses beneath that castle looked as if they were gay children sitting at the feet of a gray-bearded and granite-faced grandfather.

At the gate the travelers dismounted and joined the crowd of vagrants and tradesmen and farmers. Thanking their friendly driver, who nodded and waved good-by, the little group entered with a light step.   Werner, Hans and Melchior gazed about for a tavern, but Conrad excitedly pointed out queer sights to Elsa, who opened her eyes roundly at them.   But half of her thoughts were on finding her cousin.

She paused.　Conrad was standing, looking in rapture at a house, which bore a picture painted on its sedate front.　And, wonder on wonder, the windows were not open to the world, nor yet were they covered with oiled linen, but shone like diamonds with their tiny round panes of thick glass.

"What are these, Conrad?" asked Elsa, fixing her eyes on some strange metal affairs in a window.　Conrad tore himself away from the painting with difficulty.

"Must be instruments for use of learned astrologers," he answered.　"Those maps, charts to make a path across the sea.　My father told me the Italian, Columbus, who sailed for the Indies, discovered a new land, too, took with him some of these charts, maps, from Nürnberg."

"Ah," groaned the youth looking up again, "if I could but paint like this!　I know not, care not whatever haps, if I cannot learn to draw and paint."

The stream of people!　Turks in turbans, peasants in rustic dress with great baskets on their heads, artisans in smock and hose, soldiers pompously strutting, maidservants calling as they scrubbed the already shining steps.　Here and there were sober quack-salvers, followed by apprentices carrying their medicines in baskets.　The doctors wore long dignified robes of velvet, decked with fur, and on their feet they had pointed shoes.　So also went learned professors.　Elsa shivered with fear as she saw them.　Mountebanks capered, gypsies and beggars hurriedly plied their fraudulent trade, for well they knew that they could not stay more than two days in the city at one time, without getting a visit to the jail.

Burghers talked on corners busily, dressed in fur-trimmed doublets and fancy hose, with slashed sleeves, and feathers in their hats. The wives and daughters chattered, and tried to rival each other in silks and velvets, some with gold nets on their hair and others wearing the old-fashioned white cloth. And streets were unnaturally clean. No pigs wandered loose among the crowds.

Approaching the market square the wanderers stopped in confusion. It was a riot of color. Elsa seemed dazed, so that Hans was obliged to pull her along by the arm in order to make any progress in this press of folk.

" 'Nürnberg's hand goes through every land,' quoth the Nürnbergers, and, in sooth, I think they are right about it," exclaimed Werner, as he turned to his friends.

"But see, yonder feast garden is crowded," spoke Hans, with an eye for business, "mayhap we could get a chance to play there. Come this way," and the ponderous fellow strode off toward an inn with a hall, where fine clothed burghers and their chattering wives were gathering, obviously in holiday spirit.

"Nay, nay!" cried Elsa, stopping them with her voice, "I want not to go there, but instead to search for my kinsman, who lives near the River Pegnitz, or so my mother has told me many times."

"Then will we go there with you," said Hans quietly, turning about. But Conrad spoke.

"Nay, 'twould be foolish not to go to such inn, where they will ask you three to play. I will take the maid to her kinsman." He drew himself up with the importance of his undertaking.

"So be it," answered Hans; "then do you both meet us here when you have found him."

The musicians raised their instruments, and again turned to the inn, while Elsa called:

"Do ye care for my Fräulein, Melchior, and let her not escape in the din!"

Melchior nodded, and drew tighter the top of his bag.

"Methinks the Fräulein will add plaintive music to our strumming," commented Werner.

Elsa and Conrad made their way slowly till they came to a bridge across the river, which here flowed between over-hanging houses. After much questioning they went to try house after house, but only when they were getting tired and discouraged did they find one who knew of Herr Peter. They knocked on a door. A large woman in a cloth headdress came to their summons, but when they asked her their reiterated question she shook her head sadly.

"Alack," she said, "Herr Peter died this year agone, and his good frau has gone, with her little ones, back to her former home in some other city. But where that can be I know not."

Conrad put his hand sympathetically on Elsa's shoulder, and thanked the woman, for he could see that the maid's eyes were filling with tears, and that she was unable to speak. Turning quietly they walked forlornly back the way they had come.

"Elsa, maid, weep not, ye know ye have four of us to look out for ye. And the Fräulein too. We will not let ye come to grief."

Elsa smiled at him through her tears, and tried bravely to wipe them away.

"Yes, Conrad, I know that truly. I have my good friends—Conrad, Hans, Werner and Melchior. But methinks I want to stay in this mighty city, which seems so safe, and I want not to go to walking again where the wind is so cold, and will be colder."

"We will not go soon. Mayhap you and I can persuade our friends . . . to stay here." He looked longingly at the pictures and prints he saw displayed in a shop.

Elsa made a small face at him. "But think you they can stay in one place any time, good Conrad? I doubt it much."

The youth stopped, so suddenly that Elsa walked on a few steps before discovering that he was not beside her. She turned, amazed, and went back to him. Conrad was so still. And he was so excited about something he saw that he had not noticed that she had left him. She wheeled abruptly, and looked, frightened, into the tiny window of a shop, but all she saw there was a black and white picture of a big horse, such as one could see on the road of a morning. What was

there to give Conrad such a peculiar expression?   She
did not dare ask.

At last he spoke, confusedly, as if waking from a
daze.

"The horse!   The selfsame horse!   I liked it . . .
'twas that started me off from out the goldsmith's
house . . . 'tis the same print.   That one gave me
the idea . . . what I had always wanted."

"What is it?" asked Elsa anxiously, fearing that her
friend had suddenly gone daft, or was possessed of
some demon.

Conrad became conscious of her again.

"Why, maid, 'tis that very print that gave me the
desire to leave the goldsmith and become a painter . . .
a maker of fine prints, cut on wood . . . or on metal.
'Tis that print . . . but who the artist is I know not.
Stay!   I will ask.   No—what good—no chance have
I.   Ah—if I could."   His words poured out, confused, tumbling over each other, and ended with a
gloomy sigh.   "'Tis impossible though . . . so say
nothing more of it."

Elsa looked at him sympathetically.   She did not
know just what he meant, or what these prints and
painting were, but she wished ardently that Conrad
could do them, since he wanted to so much.   Perhaps
he wished for that as she wished for a real home again.
Elsa, also, grew sad.   And so they returned, with
miserable faces, to the square.

As the two approached the square again they heard

rollicking music, and from the inn the voice of Werner raised in song. They pushed and wormed their way through a crowd of both evil and unfortunate beggars near the door, until they came directly behind the feasting tables, spread out, and loaded with fine dishes. In front of them was the chair of a stout burgher, in a fur-trimmed jacket of velvet. His round red face beamed with good will below a fringe of curled hair.

"That must be the host. He seems to dispense viands and good cheer with a liberal hand," whispered Conrad to Elsa, who could not quite see beyond the broad back. But Conrad had already caught the eye of Hans, standing taller than the crowd as he puffed and blew shrill notes on his zinck.

Servitors ran about with dish and jug. As the burghers ate they threw to beggars—and dogs too— near the door such of the food as they could not dispose of themselves. There it was snatched and fought over until the servants were obliged to bring about order.

Elsa was growing tired and hungry. She tried to keep her place beside the youth, but she was constantly pushed away from him by the beggars, who came in closer until Elsa saw with dismay that there was a villainous looking fellow between them. He had a crooked leg. She crouched down in fear, and as she did so she suddenly saw the man, with a sly twist, turn his claw-like hand around the chair back. As it returned to him it held the pouch of the host. The fellow grinned and tried to slip through the crowd.

Elsa gave a dive between his bent legs and grasped Conrad by the ankle. The boy jumped and looked down in amazement.

"Quick, Conrad," cried the girl, "catch yon fellow with the dirty crimson doublet, for he has but now taken the purse from the host!"

Conrad slipped like a ferret through the mob, just as the large burgher discovered his loss and set up a cry for his servants, who ran about shouting, but made no headway whatsoever, since they could not tell in the noise what had been stolen or from where. There was a violent commotion near the door. The music stopped, and the three musicians grasped their staves. The servants dashed that way. By the time they reached the spot and pulled away the vagrants Conrad was holding the purse with one thin hand, but the thief had him down with the other. A knife flashed. The servants leaped on the fellow, and, after a struggle, held him fast. Conrad, rubbing his bruises, followed them to their master.

"Well done, boy, to catch a cutpurse so quickly," cried the host. "Sit you down and eat while I have my men here take this scoundrel to the magistrate."

"Nay," said Conrad breathlessly, his face flushing red, "'Twas the maid . . . she told me of the theft."

"What maid?" The stout man looked around but could see no girl.

"There behind your chair!" Conrad pointed to Elsa, who trembled with excitement, almost hidden by the tall back of the chair.

The host turned about and stared, then spoke observingly:

"Why you look like a burgher maid yourself, spite of the stained clothing, and I see that it is patched most cunningly. How comes this maid in a vagrant crowd, and how come you there too?" The musicians had edged protectingly up to Conrad and Elsa.

The youth glanced toward his friends, and observed Hans frowning at him forbiddingly, while Werner made grotesque motions with his face and hands. Conrad hesitated, then said clumsily:

"Good sir . . . maid's story be brief. A band of cutthroat thieves seized upon . . . parents. They were coming toward Nürnberg, were . . . did . . . slayed them out of hand, making off . . . all their valuables, but the maid escaped into the near-by wood . . . in furious noise. There we found her . . . promised . . . bring her thither to find her kinsman, Herr Peter. But now we are . . . were told Herr Peter be dead, and his family departed, we know not where. As for me, I . . . just a vagabond. But we would like it well . . . stay in this fine city . . . right here."

Conrad's face was crimson with unaccustomed conversation.

Elsa blushed as she listened to this strange story, but Hans looked pleased, and Werner grinned in huge amusement.

The burgher stared at them intently.

"Can I do aught for you, youth?"

"Nay," answered Conrad diffidently, "no reward do we want."

"If you would learn a trade, I might find a place for you in Nürnberg?"

"I like not . . . would not like . . . thought of a trade. An I cannot be an artist . . . painter . . . I will enter no other workshop." The youth looked stubbornly at his questioner.

The host turned to a guest seated next to him, and laughed:

"'Tis the proper artist spirit, is it not, Albrecht?"

Elsa stared at the guest. The man had a noble face, she thought, like an old religious painting, framed by long curling locks which fell gracefully about his shoulders. His dress was rich, but about it was an air of sober distinction, unlike the gaudy colored garments of town dandies. His eyes were thoughtful; and his mouth had a certain air of wistful resignation.

"Albrecht," said the stout burgher, "methinks this youth can be understood better by you than by me. Can you take him into your house as apprentice artist? I shall furnish his entrance money."

Conrad's heart flopped into his throat as a fish flops startlingly out of a basket. He felt suffocated with excitement. His face grew red then white, then red again. Elsa caught some of his joy and grew excited too. She clasped her hands tightly.

The painter smiled slowly as he looked at the two, then he said quietly:

"Yea, Wilibald, there be a place for another journey-

man in my workroom. You are at your old trick of
befriending ambitious youths. If the youth thinks
he has ability, and if he has industry, he may come.
But first I shall take him to my house to have him
show me wherein lies his belief that he may become an
artist. Be you willing to work?" turning to Conrad.

"Ah yea, master," spoke the youth in a tremble, "if
I have such a chance."

"As for the maid," continued the stout host affably,
"mayhap we might find a place in a good household
where she could help the frau." He grinned broadly
at his friend, "You could not take the girl too, Albrecht?"

The artist looked nervously from the corner of his
eye at a severely handsome woman who sat near-by.
She held her neck so stiffly that it seemed, along with
the white linen headdress above, to have been thor-
oughly starched.

"Nay, good Wilibald. We have but now had to let
our Susanna go, and the girl is too young to take her
place." He added, "My wife would not like to have
such a child, and she a vagabond too."

The woman turned an insulted face to the two
townsmen.

"Wilibald," she said in a brittle voice, "I will take
the girl. My husband cannot tell me what I want
before I have expressed my own opinion. If she be
a respectable maid, not over frivolous, she will do.
I will take her at once, and will teach her what she
needs to know, and then she will be well taught." She

rose tartly and beckoned Elsa to come with her, as if
it were already settled.　The girl moved frightened
eyes toward the stern face of her new mistress, but
they filled with distress as she looked at her four friends.
Before she could speak Hans' voice rumbled.

"Go to that home, maid.　We will miss ye sore, but
'tis a fine place for ye.　The winter would be monstrous hard for ye to wander.　Mayhap we will stay
in this fair city for a time, and see ye often."

"Oh, truly!" cried Elsa.　"Then will I go with the
kind lady.　But, Melchior, take care of your pouch,
I will get what be in it on the morrow."

Melchior nodded.

The artist looked after his wife and smiled sadly.
"What matters the means, if good works are accom-
plished," he murmured.

The host laughed, "Friend Albrecht," he chuckled,
as the woman and girl disappeared, "an if I knew you
not I would say that remark of yours was intended to
do what it did, make your Frau Agnes take the girl,
but, knowing your gentle nature, I cannot suspect you
of such guile.　However, 'twas a good ruse, intended
or not.　And you three fellows, what can I do for
you?"

"Nothing, sir, nothing," spoke Hans.　"We do
think you have done enough in providing for our
young folk.　We are old wanderers."

The burgher nodded understandingly and gave them
a handful of coins; and the three trudged away, with
a wish for good luck to Conrad, who did not look

happy at their departure.   And for men who had just
received more money than they had had in many
months the faces of the three musicians were exceed-
ingly long.

After a while Werner shrugged his shoulders, and
with a twisted little smile he sang as he walked:

". . . Red shoes the burgher goes in.
"An we have but our nosen to follow where they lead."

But his voice had lost the old joyful ring.

Said Melchior, "We be four though, not three, for
the lively Fräulein at this moment be trying to claw
the small of my back."

Hans stopped and looked about the streets.

"We will find an inn then, where the Fräulein may
come out."   They soon found the place where they
might secure a private room, which filled them with the
sensation of extreme luxury.

Leaving the kitten locked up there they descended
to the hall.   Hans, who led the way, put a big foot
across the sill, and stopped.   He thrust a hand back
quickly to hold the others, and motioned for silence.
They stood, breath suspended midway in their throats,
mouths open.   Seated on a bench, with back to the
door, was the broad figure of a red haired soldier, clad
in a buff jerkin.

CHAPTER VII

A HOME

THE house of the artist was perched on a small side hill, covering a corner, where windows on one side looked directly into a house opposite, and on the other stared fixedly across the street to a great castle wall, and far above, the towers and turrets of the Emperor's Nürnberg domain. Under the massive wall this house rested, dreaming beneath its overhanging roof, and in this roof, up four long flights of winding stairs, were two tiny dormer windows, just large enough for Elsa to gaze across at the ancient well house in the castle court, and the Animal Garden Gate Tower, round, with peaked roof. The first night she spent there, the girl sat, wrapped in her thick feather covers, when she should have been in the bed underneath them, and saw the moon glow faintly on sheer rough castle walls. There, Werner had told her, a bold bandit named Ekkelein, a hundred years ago, had escaped from his prison by springing on a horse and riding down the precipitous stone incline. Thrusting her head farther out, shivering with the chill, she would almost think that she could see those hoof prints, still said to be graven in the rock wall.

But the castle was closed now, save for servants and caretakers. No one used it except Emperor Max, who came perhaps once in several years to live for a brief time in the home of his ancestors.

The girl could smell a strong, musty odor of grain with which this topmost attic was filled, surrounding her small room with a dusty atmosphere. She heard the brazen blast of the city watchman's horn as he tooted toward the Tiergartner Gate Tower to discover if the sentinel were napping. There was a thin metallic answer blown down to the street. The footsteps of the city watchman grew fainter.

Elsa crept sleepily to bed, but felt that she had scarcely closed her eyes when she must rise again with the first gray dawn light. Her toes felt frozen, and her eyes glued together, for lack of sleep the night before. It was not yet daylight. She wondered where Fräulein Bach was as she went down the dark stairs behind the tiny flicker of a candle held in her numb hand.

Once in the kitchen she felt better, for the big stove, which had kept its warmth in spite of the death of its fiery heart during the night, made the room comfortable. Elsa warmed her chill hands, and then set about her tasks briskly; she wanted so much to do things well for these new friends. She wanted them to know that she could perform housewifely tasks even if she had been a wanderer for long.

When the sun had risen to send a pale, disgruntled light into the smoked kitchen, the girl had the early meal ready on the table, and, laid out on a tray, as her mistress had instructed her the day before, was the bread and butter and ale of the journeymen and apprentices. Elsa hoped, eagerly, that Frau Agnes might say that she was pleased. But the starched woman, swaying her voluminous skirts, merely looked at the work the girl had done, and said, crossly:

"An why is not the pewter polished?   I suppose I must get busy now and teach you the ways of a decent hausfrau."

Elsa said nothing, but swallowed a lump in her throat. She wondered if she could ever please this mistress.   And how she must work for her!

But Elsa was overjoyed when Frau Agnes called to her:

"Take that tray up to those lazy fellows above stairs, and then come down to eat your own breakfast. Afterwards I must show you the proper way to clean a room."

"Do you wish me to clean the journeymen's room above this morning?" asked the girl eagerly, for she very much wanted to find out just what were these queer things that Conrad thought so much of.

"Nay," answered the mistress, frowning, "that room

I have given up in disgust to those slovenly men.   My
husband does not want his precious things touched,
and it is of no use anyway to try, when each day brings
another load of grime into those rooms.   I clean them
but four times a year."

   Elsa went, beneath her big tray, up the stairs.   But
when she opened the door on the top floor she almost
dropped the tray.   That room was so wonderful!   All
she could see at first were the curious objects which
cluttered it.   Armor, standards with colored em-
blems of noble houses, plaster casts of people or
sections of people, porcelain vessels, shells, corals,
antlers of deer, figures of wood hung beside the
long windows, and draped with various bright
stuffs.   There was no order at all.   The room was
filled with tables and stools; at these the journeymen
were trying to work, but having a hard time subduing
their yawns.   Strange wooden frames with legs held
colored pictures, in all stages of construction.   In one
corner of the long room were two small apprentices,
engaged in grinding ink and colors in stone troughs,
and spilling a prodigious amount of both on the stained
floor.

   Not even the remarks of the journeymen on the
ancient condition of the butter which Frau Agnes be-
grudged them could take Elsa's eyes from that odd
room.

   But Conrad seemed quite at home there.   How
amazing!   He turned and saw her.

"Ah, maid, I am here to stay. Passed the test . . . Herr Dürer will give me a chance . . . prove what I can do here."

"Oh, Conrad! I am so glad. But what are those things for?"

The boy eagerly drew her in and showed her what he had so recently discovered himself. How plates made of copper were delicately engraved and printed by inking the lines, wiping the ink from their surfaces, and pressed on thin paper in a huge wooden and metal affair with a round wheel.

"Conrad, canst cut these pictures?" asked Elsa in amazement.

"Nay, not yet . . . but I will . . . I will . . . takes practice and time . . . but I will."

The journeymen laughed at his excitement, and one of them jeered at his belief.

"Wait till the master tells you 'tis nought you have done, and must all be done over," called a youth.

Elsa glared at him indignantly. Of course Conrad could do it. There was a sound from below, and a voice,

"Elsa, ye good-for-nothing. Come down and be at your work."

Elsa ran from the room, and heard some of the journeymen laugh as she went.

But this day was unreal to her. There was also the master's studio on the first floor, which she discovered with no less astonishment than she had felt on seeing the room above.

Elsa slipped in quietly, and stood stiffly near the door, so as not to touch anything valuable. It was hard to see everything at once. There was a huge window with its small glass panes, and in front of it Herr Dürer's table, with unfinished wood blocks and metal plates. For Conrad had told her that the best journeymen did the backgrounds, or some of the unimportant figures, but the master always made the faces and the larger figures. Against the walls were pictures, ready for finishing, in brilliant color. The beams above were hung with strange shells, and horns, and curious things from many lands.

There was a languid knock on the street door. Elsa sped from the studio to open it before Frau Agnes could notice. Why, it was Melchior, as long and lank as ever, and just as sleepy. He stared at her solemnly, and sniffed uncomfortably at the smell of soft soap about her.

"Maid," he said, "I know ye not. Ye have grown some years in one night."

"Ah, Melchior, are ye namesake of the Wise Man for nought? 'Tis but the town way."

"But I like it not. I like not the smell of this house neither. Methinks the folk in it must be overenergetic."

"Yea, the mistress works forever at scouring, and the master stops his work but to sleep and eat."

"I thought so." Melchior began to back toward the door, but stopped suddenly and looked confused. Frau Dürer entered with a great rustling of skirts.

The faint odor of starch came with her. Melchior
put his hand in his pouch and drew out the Fräulein,
who set up a plaintive crying. Elsa reached for her,
but the tall man held her back.

"Nay, maid. I brought her to ye, but I can see
that this crabbed woman will not let her stay."

"Ah, so I am a crabbed woman, am I? And how
know ye what I will permit?"

Melchior backed until he touched the door, and
showed signs then of trying to get out by the simple
expedient of walking through stout wooden boards,
backwards. Elsa had to answer for him.

"He but thinks, mistress, that you may not like to
have my Fräulein with you in the house. I brought
her by long roads with me here, but an you want her
not I must then think of some other way of looking
out for her."

"Well!" The woman glared at Melchior, and jingled the keys at her belt. "If ye keep her from dam-
aging the house and clawing up the napery I care not
if she stay." She stared at the tall man defiantly.

"Ah, good Frau Agnes, I do thank you. And I
promise she shall be kept well." Elsa beamed as she
took her kitten.

"But you, you bag of bones!" cried the frau to Melchior, "get from my house. And come not into it
again." Elsa gave a cry of distress, but Melchior already had fumbled open the door, and was going.
He said nothing, but as the housewife turned to leave
the room, the girl caught, with a relieved smile, a

great solemn, serious lowering of one eyelid from the thin man.   Then he was gone.

The girl hurried to the kitchen, where she found a box to put by the stove for Fräulein Bach, who ran about the floor sniffing at the furniture, and then settled down comfortably within it.   Judging from the ease with which she adapted herself to her new surroundings, Fräulein Bach had even fewer regrets than Elsa for her wandering life.

But when noon came the girl was so busy with cooking, and setting the dishes on the table, that she did not notice what the Fräulein was doing.   Drawing a breath of relief when Herr Dürer and his wife were seated before their platters, and she had heard no complaints on the food, Elsa sat down for a moment in her kitchen.   Then she thought of the cat, and looked all about for her.   She was not to be seen. Elsa looked under all the furniture, and into all of the corners, and then the paralyzing thought struck her that perhaps Fräulein Bach had escaped into the house.   She stood, rigid with fear.

There was no unusual sound from the front room. Elsa tiptoed to the door, into the hall, and across to the other door.   She opened it a crack, and peeped in. With horror she saw the small black cat, sitting on her hind legs, with her forepaws on the knee of Herr Dürer, who seemed to pay no attention, but sat, conversing quietly with his wife, who, apparently, did not suspect the presence of an extra guest.   Elsa trembled with dismay.   She must see what happened.

When Herr Dürer noticed the cat, he would probably throw her out.

Fräulein Bach wrinkled her small black nose at the smell of meat, and reached her paw up to touch, entreatingly, the hand of the master as it came down. Dürer looked at her. Then he turned back to his plate with a little smile. Elsa gasped. He was feeding the Fräulein with one hand, secretly, under the table, even as he talked to his wife. Elsa tiptoed away, leaving a crack in the door so that the Fräulein might slip out, if possible. She feared for both of the culprits should Frau Agnes find them out.

Presently in walked the Fräulein, licking her lips meditatively.

"Ye plaguey thing!" scolded Elsa, "how can ye do that when ye know so well that such a thing would send ye out of this house faster than ye came in an the frau should find out. But I guess she did not this time.

"Fräulein," continued Elsa, dropping on the floor beside her, "this is a strange household, where the mistress clacks a cross tongue, and then, as if to spite someone, she does a mighty good thing, such as taking ye in to-day. And the master, who says so little, yet manages to be kind to everyone, but as if he be afraid his Dame Agnes will find him out in it. In truth 'tis odd."

But the Fräulein, who was more inclined to take things as she found them without unnecessary comments, washed her face complacently, and went to sleep.

Elsa rose to her work again, washing up the platters, but she was interrupted by the opening door. Turning she saw, not the mistress, but the master, standing before her, looking inquiringly all about the room. Elsa curtsied, and wiped her hands on her apron.

"Where is the katze?" he asked.

Elsa pointed with a shaking finger toward the box beside the stove. Dürer walked over and looked at her with a smile.

"Bring her into my studio in a little while," he said, as he left the room.

Elsa curtsied again, but her lip was unsteady. What would he do with her? Probably throw her into the the street. She did not know whether to obey him or not. But what else could she do? Taking up the Fräulein, who yawned and looked annoyed, the girl walked with heavy steps to the studio, and handed her cat to Herr Dürer, who thanked her, and closed the door.

Elsa went back to her work, but could not keep her mind on it. And all afternoon she heard nothing from the studio, though she listened intently. When she had finished in the kitchen, and could have gone to her room to rest, she still stayed there, with the door open, listening.

When she had entirely given up hope of ever seeing the Fräulein again, came that lady importantly, as if it were no concern of hers for Elsa to worry about her. The girl leaped up and ran to the kitten.

"Fräulein," she whispered, sitting on the floor beside

her, "why did he keep ye so long?   What did he want ye in there for?   Why I thought he did not like ye and had thrown ye out.   What was it?"

But the Fräulein gazed back at her inscrutably, then crawled into her lap and began to purr.   Elsa rubbed her head.

"Ah, I wish you would tell me, Fräulein Bach."

But Fräulein Bach, who had kept so many of Elsa's secrets, proved once more her powers of discretion.

Chapter VIII

RED FEATHERS FLY

Hans, Werner and Melchior lodged disconsolately in their room at the Silver Duck Inn. Hans slumped stolidly, trying to think; Melchior's long form lay stretched on the bed, apparently asleep; but Werner darted about the room, his coat billowing out behind him, until, in a fit of irritation at his lack of fruitful ideas, he snatched the offending garment from his shoulders and flung it at a chest.

"Strike me for a loon if we are not the sorriest mess of vagabonds, who cannot even discover how to dispose of a cowardly soldier."

"He be cowardly only when his weapons are taken from him," spoke Hans from his corner, "and that they are not now. Here we have been, eating and sleeping since yestreen, never leaving the room, except for Melchior's little trip out to-day, and that he managed right cleverly. But here we sit, and good busi-

ness waits without, coins clink in the market place,
and times are ripe for entertainment."

"Yea," fumed Werner, rubbing his round brow as
if he would punish it for their distress.   "And not an
idea among us.   What if he should see Elsa by chance?
She would get short shrift from his master."

Melchior turned over on his face and the round blue
eyes of Hans grew more vacant.

"Ah!" shouted the little fat man, halting by the window.   "I have it."   He bounced to the chest, drew
his cloak about him importantly, set his hat at a dignified angle upon his brow, and cried gleefully:

"Do ye both wait here for a time, till I be with you
again, and stir not from the doorway.   I have a plan
at long last.   I'll soon be back."   He strutted into
the passage, with a strange and peculiar step, very
solemn, very pompous, and withal a bit mysterious.
Hans turned his head and Melchior rose from the bed
to stare.

"Now why," said the lank fellow wonderingly, "did
that idiot go off so cocksurely?   I will see what he
looked at so closely in the yard."

"Nought but a red rooster, and a passing lean and
mangy one at that," said Melchior in a melancholy tone
as he returned to his bed.

The inn kitchen was almost deserted at this early
hour of the afternoon, for the evening's trade had not
yet begun to fill the long rough table in the tap room,
nor yet the settles in the kitchen.   There was the cook,
busy at her stove, and a smudgy pot boy, cleaning earth-

enware steins.   The landlord stood at one side laughing good-naturedly with a guest, who presently tipped his stein bottom up and departed.   The pot boy disappeared.   The inn-keeper turned and saw a strange little man seated on a settle by the stove.   He looked at him curiously, for the fellow sat upright and gazed before him, as if the profound secrets of life were unfolding themselves to him one by one, but very completely.   And once in a while he nodded at some invisible conversationalist.

The inn-keeper opened his wide mouth to make a jolly remark, but just as he did so he caught a glimpse of his guest's mystic gaze.   The host stood, with jaw still hanging.   Then he closed it with a snap, but remained uneasy, he knew not why.

"Why came ye here?" he asked.

A deep voice, fraught with the weight of mysterious knowledge, rose to him from the depths of the guest's being,

"Man hath need of the heavenly angels to keep devils from his door."

The inn-keeper jumped, and dropped a knife.

"Place not a knife with blade up, for so you do cut the fingers of angels.   Man hath need of the heavenly angels to keep devils from his door."

The fat man backed hurriedly toward the window, and screwed his head toward it, taking his gaze with a jerk from the guest.   His hand went nervously toward his chin.

"Point not at the moon by day," quoth the voice,

"for such practice doth injure the eyes of angels. Man hath need of the heavenly angels to keep devils from his door."

The host shook like a jelly. He backed toward the door, and in doing so knocked a pot to the floor with a great clatter of copper.

"Cast not metal upon the floor, for so ye do deafen the ears of angels. Man hath need of the heavenly angels to keep devils from his door.

"There was an inn-host who cut the fingers of angels. They left his house. Devils came in. They shriveled him till he blew away in a high wind like a grain husk on the breeze." He waved his hand mysteriously. "There was an inn-keeper who injured the eyes of angels. They ceased to look down on him. An imp came and filled his eyes with sand till he wept himself into a puddle of water, and stayed in the road for pigs to wallow in." He moved his arm solemnly upward. "There was an inn-owner who deafened the ears of angels. A band of devils came and hung on his ears till they drooped to the floor, and tangled in his legs, and threw him down, and grew around him, coiled like two snakes, and wrapped him forevermore in a living tomb." He was silent.

The fat host dropped to his knees, as if they had given way beneath him. His head bobbed up and down like a small boat on a monstrous sea.

"Master, good master, save me!" he cried.

"Do ye know who I be?"

"Nay, but save me, good master, save me!"

The guest rose to his fullest inches, drawing his blue cloak about him tightly, with a regal flourish.

"I am a worker in white magic, for the good of mankind. I disrupt the activities of devils, and know all the saintly ways of angels. I am come to relieve your house of a demon."

On the floor the inn-keeper jabbered his thanks alone, for the frowsy cook had long since fled.

"How know ye there be a demon here?"

"Man hath need of the heavenly angels to keep devils from his door. Come!" He stalked into the yard. The host followed as fast as his shaky legs would carry him.

"Devils come in many and varied shapes. I will show you, by magic means, what shape the devil will assume."

The inn-keeper's eyes stood out, frog-like.

His solemn guest looked about the barnyard, with the animals, who were unconcernedly pecking and grunting. He found a long stick. He held the stick up straight, then bent it down, then laid it on the ground and murmured strange words over it, in a gutteral tone:

> "Devil come, Devil go,
> Worry not the inn-host so,
> Take your form of mortal foe,
> Ishka-dishka-gander-cock,
> Swine-ox-horse-cow-skillybock."

The inn-keeper's teeth chattered in his head like the rattle of hail on cobble stones.

The mysterious stranger whirled and bounded into the air, and sputtered and shouted, and whispered and pranced.   Then he picked up the stick and drew a big circle in the dust.   Taking from his pouch some whitish crumbs, which mightily resembled ordinary bread, he threw them in the circle with a flourish of his arm. The host expected to see brimstone and sulphur rise in a cloud from his yard, but nothing happened.   He watched, breath suspended.

A scrawny red rooster came running up and began to peck at the magic crumbs.   The stranger, who stood perfectly still as the fowl advanced, wheeled and pointed his finger at the bird.

"Nought can save ye now.   Ye have morally offended your guardian angel, which sits, invisible, on your hearth.   Man hath need of the heavenly angels to keep devils from his door!"

"Ah, save me, save me, good and worthy master!"

"In the form of a cock comes the devil.   He may be already within your doors."

The host was almost a jibbering idiot now.   Even his words could not be distinguished.   Only his cries rang about the yard.

"Ah!   Ah!   Ah!   Ah!"

The guest walked close to him, and pointed a finger into his face.

"I can save ye, but only if ye do as I say."

"Yea, yea, ah, ah, ah!"

The guest drew him into the house, where he shuddered violently, and fell to a bench.   The visitor sat before him and held his eye with a gaze full of power.

"Know ye, this devil comes in the shape of a man, but he is really a red cock?   Catch ye the bird in the yard.   Cook it in its feathers, gently so as not to disturb the plumage.   Canst do this?"

"Yea, good and lordly master," mumbled the man.

"Hearken to me then, carefully.   Know ye that a devil which inhabits a red cock is the most malignant devil of all the fiery crew?"

The host clasped his trembling hands.

"But he can be caught at the moment when he admits that he is a red rooster.   There are magic ways to do this."

"What, ah what ways?"

"Put this cooked bird on a big wooden trencher. Find a large bow and an arrow.   Thrust the arrow through a wing of the bird, and place the bow, with string outspread, around the cock.   For the red cock devil be doomed to take the shape of a man when he has been shot by an arrow.   That is his punishment, and he cannot go back to his home with Lucifer till he works manifest evil on a household, and becomes a red cock again."

The inn-host covered his face with his hands.

"But when he sees this trencher, so adorned, he will be angered terribly, and will admit that he is a cock."

"Ah, ah, he will kill us all."

"Nay, not so.   When the trencher be set before him then ye must cry:

"Hast ever been shot,
For deer or cock?"

"The man who grows angered at table is the devil."

"Ah, master, what to do then?"

"Then will I have brought in two stout fellows who will overpower him and truss him up. For his evil powers be confounded then."

There was a strange air of fear about the Inn of the Silver Duck that evening, as guests began to arrive in the big front room, where one long table was supplied for them. There were but few visitors that night, for the weather was bad. A feeling of oppression, such as one feels when the air is still, not a leaf moves, but a quality of emptiness presages approaching storm, hung over the dark room. Rain fell mournfully from the eaves outside. Even the surly pot boy looked fearfully into corners as he moved about. The fat inn-keeper was one moment red with activity, and the next white with anxiety.

He peeped into the front room. There were but five guests there. The queer stranger was not visible. A peasant farmer and his stout wife sat stolidly waiting for food. A priest in a black robe extended bare feet to the stove. Two youthful travelers, foreign artisans no doubt, leaned against huge wine barrels in a corner. They moved to the bare, rough table, as if by unspoken agreement, when they saw the host appearing with a big trencher held high.

"Our good host trembles like a man who goes to be wed. What ails him?" whispered one of the travelers.

"What does it matter, so long as he brings food?"

answered his companion. But the five pairs of eyes stared amazed at the dish displayed in the center of the long table. It was a bird, cooked in all its plumage, and what a scrawny red bird!

There was not a sound. The host, who shook like a bare tree in a wintry breeze, gazed from one to the other. There was nothing but blank amazement on every face. He whispered in a doomed voice:

> "Ha-has-hast ever-r-r been shot-t-t,
> For deer-r-r or co-co-cock?"

He drew a breath of huge relief. There was no angry word, not even a recognizable furious expression on any of these five faces. But his breath stopped half-way in his throat. His jerkin was grasped from behind, and a rough, bellowing voice boomed in his ear. If ever he heard anger this was it.

The shuddering man looked up into the face of a guest who had arrived a little late. It was a great, bullying countenance, framed in flaming red hair.

"Red cock? Who makes merry with my name? You worm, you crawling, filthy pig!"

A great hairy hand shook the stout man until he danced a grotesque arabesque with his toes barely touching the floor, and his face screwed into a gargoyle mask. His eyes stood out like bursting grapes. He could not even gasp. Then, with a sudden heave of anguish, the wretched fellow wrenched his jerkin from his captor's grasp and stumbled into the dark passage. The fiery Cock followed at top speed, with a noise as of ten horses pounding across a wooden bridge.

The terrified guests in the tap room jumped. With the sound of a clap of thunder the big bowsman hit the floor. Three dark shapes were all over him, pounding, thumping, bumping. His loud and strenuous curses were abruptly subdued into clothy mumblings as something was tied over his raging mouth. His hands and legs were secured. He was suddenly shrouded in a huge piece of sacking.

Three pairs of arms lifted the enormous package and carried it, not without protest from two of them, into the covered alley beyond the door. The night was black and furious.

"Now what to do?" asked the tallest of the three men, "for it rains apace, and I like not going through streets in it."

"Wait," whispered the small round man, bounding into the wet street. Presently he returned with a lumbering cart, drawn by an ox, who gazed at the excited humans with a large disillusioned eye. Behind him was a driver, stupid and dripping, who looked as uninquiring as his beast.

The large tied bundle was placed carefully in the empty cart, and covered with a pile of straw filched from the barnyard behind. The driver received three coins, and drove off slowly, jolting on the wet stones, looking as if he delivered such packages to the countryside every night of his life.

The three men hurried within, and found the host,

shining with relief and perspiration, getting the furniture back into place.

"We must go from here," whispered one of the three to his companions, "Red Cock might return."

The small man, solemn and mysterious again, folded his wet cloak about him and advanced to the host, who stared at him with a scared face.

"How much do I owe you, inn-host, with my two friends?"

"Ah, nay, nay, ye owe me nothing," said the fat man, "'tis I who be in your debt. If ye be going," he looked relieved, "then take, with my compliments, a horn of fine wine with each of you."

The mysterious stranger moved his hand slowly, raising his short arm, until the company, with its twelve eyes following together, seemed to see it grow almost long enough to touch the blackened beams, so portentous was the gesture. He brought it down from aloft in a large circle, and muttered some unintelligible sounds as he did so. Then he drew his cloak tighter, bowed low, and said:

"Man hath need of the heavenly angels to keep devils from his door!"

As the three walked up the street in the pouring rain, the tall, lank one muttered:

"'Tis unnatural to go out in such a weather. Why could we not stay there for nothing till day?"

"Nay," answered the fat man, "I was bottled up like a jar of the Black Man's brimstone broth, which with a little waiting might blow off with a noise like thunder. And there's no magic in that."

CHAPTER IX

ART IS LONG

THE old house of the artist echoed with noises, from the topmost floor to the ground. The third story laughed with the voices of young men and boys, silly, joyous; the clash of metal plates dropped; the grinding of colors in stone troughs; the soft thud of wood. Oftentimes there would come the scuffle of boots and hard breaths of tussling youths, promptly silenced by a harsh woman's voice from below.

The second floor, which held the rooms of the artist and his wife, and the print room, groaned and rattled and complained with the labor of the press, and the footsteps of the older journeymen, as they worked with prints or paints and wooden panels.

The ground floor mingled strangely the noises of pots and pans, kettles and platters, from the dark kitchen at the rear, with quiet but insistent sounds of work from the studio of the master, which was placed at the other side of the little hall. And through the whole creaking house rang the shrill, commanding tones of the mistress, always subduing, yet never rendering unnoticeable, the quiet, kind voice of the master.

Equally evident were the odors of this divided household. Paint and polish! Ink and hot water! Oils and cooking fat! Turpentine and roasting meats! Heated metals and soft soap!

On a day in December, Elsa, feeling vastly important, for was not this the first occasion on which her severe mistress had consented to send her to market alone, put coins in her pouch, and took a basket on her arm.

She smoothed her neat dress, carefully patted her starched white headdress, which gave her the appearance of a small, winged bird, and went below stairs to do her errand. As she came down she was almost shoved on her nose by the crowd of apprentices and journeymen, who came running, with a noise like a herd of wild boars, at her. She drew to one side, offended at their rudeness, but they did not even notice her wounded feelings. Elsa called after them curiously, for they wore caps and coats:

"Where be going, that ye all try to topple me down the stairs in your haste?"

"To the Guild meeting," shouted one as they scuttled into the street. Elsa looked after them, but did not see Conrad.

She was ready dressed in her mantle, and was passing

through the hall on her way out when she saw that
the studio door was ajar.   Remembering swiftly that
Herr Dürer was already in town, and that Dame Agnes
was visiting with a neighbor, the girl hesitated a moment, even as she wished to go in.   She had, for a long
time, wanted to see closely the strange things in that
room.   She peeped in through the crack.   There was
Fräulein Bach, curled up among painty rags and tiny
porcelain jars on the table.

"Welladay, if ye do not look as if ye own the place,"
exclaimed the surprised girl.   "Methinks ye are mighty
familiar with the master's things.   But I had better
get ye out before Dame Agnes returns."

She moved cautiously into the room, and picked up
the sleepy cat, but when she reached the door again she
was compelled by her curiosity to return and look.
Hanging from the beams of the low ceiling, blackened
with age, were strange fruits.

There were cocoanuts from the wild islands of the
South, bone saws from queer fish of the outlying seas,
horns of fierce animals, and odd trinkets brought by
Herr Dürer's father from Hungary.

"Now what do ye suppose this is for, Fräulein
Bach?" asked Elsa, puzzled, as she gazed at a table
which held a small group of queer gray ridges.   "Why,"
she cried suddenly, "'tis a tiny fortress.   There be a
wall all around, with a castle within, and a moat and
a gate and a drawbridge.   Do you suppose the master
made it?

"There, Fräulein, be the beginnings of a fine picture,

and the paint is put on with oils on a piece of wood."
She was rather glad that Conrad was not there to con-
tradict her. "It has a beautiful lady, who must be the
Madonna, and see the Child! What is that in the
corner? Why, Fräulein," said the girl in astonishment, "'tis a picture of you! Welladay! Now I know
why the master likes to have ye in here with him."
But the kitten looked at it without surprise; in fact
she seemed a bit bored. But then, no doubt, she had
seen it before.

Elsa wished that she might take up one of the strange
long sticks, painted in bright colors, and dab the end,
which was a tuft of fine hair, into the paints she saw
spread out in little soft mounds on a board. But she
did not dare touch anything.

She went and sat in the window seat to look into the
street. There was the faint sound of a bagpipe coming in from the town. The music reminded her of her
three friends, which, in turn, made her wonder what
had happened to them.

"Why have they not let me know, Fräulein, what
they be doing? 'Tis queer, and unlike them too.
Methinks they must be angry for the harsh words
Frau Agnes said to Melchior." She sighed sadly, but
could think of no way to find them.

There was the sound of hasty footsteps coming
through the front room. Elsa jumped up guiltily.
She heard the master in the hall speaking to his wife.
Her voice rang angrily. Elsa dared not brave the
wrath of Frau Agnes. She slipped behind a tall pic-

ture which stood in a corner, and she heard Herr Dürer
say:

"Wife, I care not for the thought of having others
hear what you have to say.   Come in here, where we
can shut the door."

Elsa heard the steps advance into the studio, and
those of his wife follow.   The girl did not want to
overhear their quarrel, but neither did she like to come
out from her hiding-place.   So she smoothed the fur
of the Fräulein, and remained where she was.

"Albrecht," snapped Frau Agnes, twirling her
bunch of keys until they jingled a little tune, "have I
no rights as a wife, when you go so far as to take an important commission more than a month agone, and
tell me nought of it?   Have you no consideration for
me, a weak woman, that you agree to do one of the
finest paintings that you have ever undertaken for a
noble, and say not a word to me about it till now?   I
tell you I'll have some rights."

"Agnes," murmured the distraught artist's voice,
"I thought it a fair price, and agreed to finish it for
him by Lent.   It was an interesting painting to do, a
small wood panel for his new chapel.   The chance
caught my fancy."

"Yea, caught your fancy, but not your purse strings
I'll warrant.   You took it because you wanted to do
the picture.   You did not think of the fact that we all
have to have food, and lay up something for our old
age too.   When those lazy journeymen do nothing but
eat their heads off."

Dürer said nothing.

"How much did you agree to get for this painting?"

"A hundred gulden."

"One hundred gulden," the woman's voice was violent, "you agreed to do all of this work for one hundred gulden, and he a rich noble, and you could have gotten at least two hundred or even three!" She lowered her voice. "But you will send a messenger to him at once and demand more."

"Nay," he said quietly, "I will not. And neither will you. I agreed to do it at that price, and thus it stands." Elsa heard his hand fall on the table, and then the crash of some small object that he must have brushed from it. Footsteps retreated from the room.

There was no sound below until his steps, weary and forlorn, died away upstairs. Then the frau rushed to the kitchen with a great rustling of starchy petticoats. The house was quiet.

Elsa crept out nervously and remembered with a gasp that she must go to the market place. She dropped the kitten and slipped noiselessly through the front room and so into the street.

The air seemed sweet to her face, though it was cold, as she plodded carefully through the snow down Zisselstrasse toward the market square.

Past the small crooked houses, looking pinched and huddled in the chill, she went, and sniffed eagerly at the smell of sausage meats coming from a tiny shop which leaned against, and seemed part of, a big and impressive hall. There was one small window, like a solemn eye, looking out of the front of the shop at her. It reminded her somehow of Melchior, and at that thought she lost the fear that had troubled her, and laughed. The River Pegnitz was dreary now, and Elsa was glad when she arrived at the market, with its booths set up in the snow, and could walk among them.

Passing back with her purchases she happened to look into the window of a baker's shop on a side street.

Why, that was uncommonly like Hans, but how could it be?

The girl stopped short and peered in through a tiny frosted pane.

"Cousin Hans," she cried, bursting into the little shop, "glad am I to see ye again! How came ye here?"

The baker brushed a floury hand across his hair, and stared a moment. Then he ran from behind his table and grasped her by both hands, shaking them up and down vigorously as he did so.

"Maid, and glad am I too."

"But, Hans, why have ye left me there for these many days agone, and never a sight nor sound of ye? I do think it unkindly of ye."

"Ah, maid," the baker's blue eyes looked distressed, and his calm took on a faintly apologetic air. "Ah, maid, we thought between us that ye were so respectably placed that 'twere better leave ye be, and not ruin your chances by having three vagabonds hang about the door. Ye are neat as noodles now, no longer a waif maid."

"Yea, good Hans, and that I be too still. Oh, but I be glad to see ye, and so will Conrad be glad when I tell him of it, for we have both missed ye all sorely."

Hans folded his big fists importantly on his middle and looked pridefully about his shop.

"Here I be, maid, respectable as a wife a-sitting in her kitchen. Assistant to a fine baker I be, for I like not the thought of a bitter cold wind in my face an I be roadward bound."

"'Tis well, but how did ye get this place?"

"As ye knew, maid, I had some experience apprenticed to a baker once. But no such thought entered my noddle this time. 'Twas chance, who rules most of my doings.

"I was a-walking down the street thinking on many things, but chiefly on the absence of coins in my purse. And Melchior and Werner were likewise plucked bare, for we share and share alike. The geld we plucked from our music at the feast of Wilibald Pirkheimer had melted away, overmuch fast too, but we did not know why. I was a-walking down the street thinking of these things, for Melchior and Werner had gone separate ways from me, looking for chances to give entertainment. The people seemed not in holiday mood.

"I came to a corner, where rain and snow had made a puddle of muddy slush as big as a wine barrel, but not nearly so warming. There were some folk standing about shouting, and so I joined the crowd, shivering against the wind. On either side of the puddle were two stout fellows holding the ends of a long pole, and swung from the center of this branch was a big withe basket, which was being dipped up and down in the icy water."

"Why would they dip a basket up and down in a puddle?" asked the girl, mystified.

"Why, for no reason that I could see, unless for exercise. But I almost forgot to tell ye that in the basket was a squirming, wriggling creature, a fellow dressed in the white of a baker's rig. Each time he came up from the water he yelled, and each time he went under he splashed mud hither and yon.

" 'What's this?' I called to one of the long-legged pole holders. 'Wherefore dip a fellow in a puddle on an icy day like this? Why not drop him in River Pegnitz, and save all the sputter?'

"Standing beside me was an old pouchy man, also in baker's costume. He seemed to be directing the proceedings.

" 'Sir,' he answered me, his face red and puffy, 'this piece of scum was assistant in my bake shop, and I caught him cheating a customer for his own gain. This be the way Nürnberg punishes dishonest bakers.'

"Presently they lowered the basket, the creature crawled out amid jeers from the folk around about, and made off down the street as fast as his drenched legs would carry him, muttering curses between chattering teeth.

"So here I be, hired in his place, and finding the life not bad. At least 'tis warm and well fed and com-

fortable—save for the pesky flour, which gets in
my beard."

"But where be Werner, and our energetic Melchior?"
asked Elsa, looking pleased. "Tell me not they have
jobs too?"

"Yea, Werner has gone back to his old trade of
cobbling, and likes it much, since he is assistant to
Master Hans Sachs. He it was who drove us into the
gate of Nürnberg among the hides. Methinks he
hired our explosive friend more for his songs than for
his cobbling. And, marry, that shop do be filled to
the echo with noises, first the rap rap of tools, then the
clack clack of song. They do say Werner is a fit as-
sociate for Master Sachs, being somewhat of a poet
himself."

"Welladay! I am glad to hear these things, for I
had hoped that you would all stay here in this fine
city too. But what of our namesake of the Wise
Man?"

Hans shook his head mournfully,

"We got him a place with an inn-keeper, but he
went to sleep while drawing wine for the guests, and
let a whole cask waste itself upon the floor. In truth
he might have drowned in wine that day, but from
the outside, not from the inside. So the keeper ousted
him right speedily.

"Then we got him into a rich merchant's house as
a porter, but he was so slow about his labor that he took
all day to carry a roll of velvet across town, and when
he got there about dark the burgess who ordered it had

taken a roll elsewhere. She sent it back, which Melchior said was passing hard on him to have to take the
pestiferous thing back after carting it like an ox all
the way over there. He arrived at his shop the next
morning, having taken the velvet to his inn and slept
with his head on it all night. The merchant kicked
him out and paid him nothing.

"With great effort we found a place for him as cook
in a household, but when the food came upon the table
he had placed, through accident, salt in the pudding
and sugar in the broth. He got not even a meal from
that house, since he could not eat his own victuals.

"Then Werner got him, through the intercession of
Hans Sachs, a place as assistant to the chief chirurgeon
of Nürnberg town. This, we thought, will suit him
well, for the food be good and the work light, and even
a daft fellow can fail not in carrying about, at the heels
of a quacksalver, a basket of medicals and ungents.
'Twas but a day he lasted there, for the idiot went with
his master to see a dame who had a vapor, and when the
chirurgeon bade him give the lady a potion com-
pounded of violet water and orange leaves, he poured
down her a draught of pepper and brimstone which
caused the dignified dame to rise from her couch and
caper into the street in a manner most unbecoming a
gentle lady.

" 'In faith,' said our Melchior, ''tis overmuch ef-
fective,' thinking he had cured the dame. But the
chirurgeon threw the basket at him, leeches, bottles
and all, and our lank one was once more out of a job."

Hans sighed dolefully, as Elsa grinned.

"Now we can get him no other, so he sleeps and eats all day in a tavern and Werner and I must pay.   With a curse on the clumsy fool!"   The big man shook his whiskers, but Elsa saw a twinkle in his erstwhile solemn blue eyes.   She laughed.

"Methinks our Melchior be cleverer than he looks."

"And are ye happy in that big house, maid?" inquired Hans suddenly.

"Yea, good cousin.   Sometimes I get overmuch weary, with all that the frau puts upon me to do, but I do think she likes me, withal that she never shows it. But the thing that makes me angry with her is the way she treats Herr Dürer.   He is, indeed, a patient man.   She will throw violent words at him, but he says nothing, and then she will bake with her own hands a fine cake just for him.   If she had not such a tongue in her head she would indeed be a comfortable frau."

"Yea," said Hans with another twinkle, "there is nought wrong with her but her disposition, I ween. 'Tis the sole fault of a snapping dog too."

"But, Hans, I am afraid no longer of the Red Cock, and," her voice lowered fearfully, "his master.   I think he cannot find me here."

"Yea, maid, ye are safe now."   But Hans thought of a certain red rooster, and he thought also that if the fighting bird returned things might go hard with them all.   But, since he had not returned, perhaps he and his master had found fatter witch-hunting elsewhere.   Nevertheless Hans could not help but remember the anger of the Cock at the trick they had played on him, and he had a strong suspicion that the fellow had but gone for his master before returning to their city of Nürnberg.

Elsa walked thoughtfully up the hill to the house near the Thiergartnerthor.   She slipped within the big door, and left her heavy basket in the kitchen.

"The place be uncommonly quiet," she wondered, "all the 'prentices and journeymen have not returned, I ween.   Mayhap Conrad might be above stairs, for he would always flee a meeting for a chance to work."

She went slowly up the steps, and entered the studio of the journeymen.   As she came into the big untidy room she saw the youth seated at his bench, with his hair falling, unnoticed, into his eyes.   Elsa sat in a corner, and looked with interest at Conrad, who, though so intent on his work, yet found time to lift his head and smile at her.   So the girl sat looking and the boy sat working until a noise on the stairs drew their attention.

The returning youths rushed into the room, letting in with the opening door a burst of laughter which was hushed as Herr Dürer followed.

"To work now.   Ye have had time enough off today.   I know not what to do with such lazy fellows." But the gentleness of his eyes softened the sting of his words.   He moved over to Conrad.

"What is this?"   Looking over his shoulder.   "What be doing here?"   He frowned suddenly.

Conrad stood, his face crimson.

"Master," he stammered, "I . . . I . . . did but . . . want to work with wood . . . stead of metal—"

"Know ye not," said Dürer severely, "this is not the way to work this wood? How came you to do this?"

Conrad trembled. Elsa bit her lower lip tightly. There was a snicker from one of the journeymen.

Conrad's tongue clung to the roof of his mouth, until in the heavy silence he managed to bring it back to speech.

"Master, I saw many times . . . the journeymen worked on copper engraving . . . I tried . . . tried but knew not much about it . . . saw them so easily . . . I thought . . . might be easier for me to work with one of these wood blocks . . . meant not to ruin it."

"How came ye to know what tool to use, or how?"

"Karl, here," he pointed to a big journeyman, the fellow who had snickered, "Karl, I asked if I could do the same work on wood as on copper. He told me yea, but knife must be used . . . not an engraver as on metal . . . knife for the wood. This I tried to do." He looked down at his feet.

Dürer stared at Karl a moment. The fellow's grin slowly faded as he met the look, and he nervously fingered a corner of his blue blouse.

Dürer picked up the carved block and gazed at it quietly. Then he walked slowly to the ink stone and rolled the ink out thinly with the leather dabber. This he pushed across the block, until it was evenly covered. There was a thick silence. The journeymen looked frightened.   Then the sound of a sniffle from a small apprentice broke the tense atmosphere.

"Come here, Conrad," commanded the master.

The youth went to him.

"Bring me a piece of thin paper."

He carefully fitted the paper over the inked block of wood, and rubbed the back of the paper with a small strip of walrus tusk until the reverse side of the paper was black with ink which had come through. Then he peeled the paper off, and showed the right side of the picture to Conrad, who had spent the day cutting it.

The boy gasped in amazement.   The face and hands of the knight he had made were as black as if he had drawn a Nubian.   The sky was dark, and the trees and armor of the knight were white.

"Master," he exclaimed distressfully, "what can have happened?   I made it not that way.   It be backwards."

The artist smiled.   A twinkle took possession of his eyes.

"Yea, Conrad," he said slowly, "that is because you did work as if it were on metal.   On copper you do engrave lines, which hold the ink, and you rub off the surfaces, leaving on paper the lines you make black in the cutting.   But on wood 'tis the other way.   The ink be on the uncut surfaces, so they come black, and the lines be white.   This must be done by reversing the drawing."

"Ah, master," groaned the youth, "I be terribly ig-

norant.   And this block be ruined.   And 'tis fine pear
wood!   Ye will not . . . let me . . . stay on now
here . . . so stupid . . . silly."

Herr Dürer placed his hand gently on Conrad's
shoulder.

"Conrad, this is a fortunate mistake for you.   Now
you know that to learn you must make mistakes.   But
next time take not the word of Karl, for his jokes are
funny but to himself.   Choose another smooth block,
and do you this again in reverse.   Cut out what you
want to be white, instead of what you want black.
For methinks you do show unusual ability for a be-
ginner.   Henceforth, when you have perfected the
art somewhat, I shall let you do the work in wood, since
you like it, and take up metal graving later."

He walked from the room, and, as the girl joyfully
followed him down the stairway, she saw him shrug
his velvet-clad shoulders in a foreign fashion which
he had picked up in Italy, or in some other far-off land
he had visited, she supposed.   And she heard him
give a low chuckle.

CHAPTER X

CHAIN OF GOLD

WINTER'S cold still enveloped the city, and folk stuffed their big tile stoves until they sent warm fingers to search out every corner of the rooms. Not yet were the bath houses on River Pegnitz filled to overflowing with people, but, though all the world was dreary out of doors, still there was a faint feeling of finality about the chill.

Elsa rose one day long before the dawn, her heart in a fever of excitement. This was to be a big day. There were many things to do about the house on this Sabbath before going off, stiff and pious, to church. And then, then in the afternoon she was to see the glorious, the much talked-of contest of the Meistersingers. For the two-hundred and fifty Meistersingers of Nürnberg were, on this day, to hold a singing contest among those of their number who wished to try out for the Master Rank. Elsa knew that they must pass a trial to become members of their song Guild, and to do this they had to sing a song perfectly. Werner was already one of them.

But to become a Master in the Guild a singer must write his own poem, put it to his own music, and sing it with no more mistakes in rule than seven. This must be done before both the Guild and the folk of the town in St. Catherine's Church. Elsa's head whirled at the thought of such bewildering things, and for Werner too.

She was on tiptoe with expectation. For weeks before the great event she had planned to go, ever since she had heard that Werner would sing; she had asked permission, and had shaken in her shoes lest her mistress take a notion to keep her at home. Now it was the week before Lent, and the great day for the Meister-singers.

Elsa dressed hurriedly and shivered down the cold stairway to her big kitchen, where there were still a few glowing coals in the stove. The Fräulein, now much grown, and looking a mysterious black shadow in the dim light of Elsa's candle, rose and stretched herself, as she blinked up at her friend. The girl rubbed the fur a bit, and heard it pop and snap.

"In faith, Fräulein Bach, an the Red Cock could hear those noises from your fur he would never dare touch ye." She sat down to tell the cat of her new farthingale, and new mantle too, which Frau Dürer had given her unexpectedly but a week ago.

"Fräulein, I wish I could take ye to hear the singers

and our Werner, for he be the finest singer in the world, and will win the highest rank I doubt not at all."

But there was work to do. Elsa set about her tasks, and soon had the fire roaring and the pots boiling. But then, wondering if Conrad had yet risen, and thinking that he must be already up and wanting a bite to eat, she slipped a slice of bread and butter beneath her apron and crept noiselessly toward the stairs. When the girl came from the kitchen and was passing the door she heard a thumping and bumping on the steps, and knew, with a shiver of dismay, that the Frau was descending. And well Elsa had been taught by her mistress that on no occasions were the journeymen to receive more food than she sent to them. Elsa looked about and then stepped back into the dark and invitingly open doorway of the kitchen. Fortunately she had not lighted a candle.

There was a tiny taper glow moving jerkily down the stairs, around the bend, and to the first floor. Elsa could make out a dark, wide shape with flaring white headdress behind it. The girl stood quietly in the dark doorway. Frau Agnes went into the studio across the way. Presently Elsa saw the candle placed on a bench near the big cabinet inside, where Herr Dürer was wont to keep some of his finished pictures. Clumsy fingers which seemed to strive to be silent were pushing back the doors. Elsa saw, as she could not forbear moving forward to look, the wife draw forth a pile of wooden panels, examine them closely with the dim light, then place them again within. She was reaching for another pile.

The girl wondered curiously why Frau Agnes chose such an unseemly hour to look at pictures which she must have seen before, but she was afraid by a movement to attract attention to her guilty self, with the bread.

The woman looked long at a painting, which had been placed carefully in a corner of the cabinet, then she sighed as if satisfied, concealed it under her big apron, and creaked out and up the stairs. Elsa drew back and waited some minutes, which seemed hours to her, before she slipped back into the kitchen and replaced her slice of bread in its crock. Cocks were crowing. It was day. Her thoughts ceased to ponder the mystery, and turned themselves excitedly toward the Church of St. Catherine and the afternoon.

But, later in the morning, she thought of the queer actions of her mistress when she looked from an upstairs window and saw Frau Agnes bowing ceremoniously from her door a richly dressed merchant, whose carriage and horses, with gaudy driver, waited at the corner. For, of a certainty, the good frau acted very strangely. She curtsied and smiled at the man, and bent in frequent bows, the while she chattered to him. And she took some glittering coins into her hands. Elsa caught a few words, disconnected.

"Best colors money can buy . . . no better . . . camel's hair brushes used—of the finest . . . expensive oils . . . much work." The merchant seemed pleased, as he carried away under his arm a big package, wrapped in linen.   And yet Frau Agnes glanced often back toward the door, even as she smiled, and looked, Elsa thought, as if she were afraid someone might come out.   The man drove off.

All the forenoon before the contest Frau Agnes smiled and smiled to herself when she thought no one looked her way.   Finally, when they had all returned from church, Herr Albrecht noticed this unaccustomed state of affairs, and, letting his curiosity gain the better of his caution, he said amiably,

"Good wife, you are in fine feather to-day.   Is't the weather, or the Sabbath, or the Meistersinger contest this even?"

She scowled at him, as the sun suddenly hides behind a dark cloud.

"Nay, Albrecht, 'tis but my own good humor.   Cannot a wife look pleasant an she choose?"

"Yea, certainly.   But who were those fellows in livery who waited before our house this morning? Why were they here on the Sabbath?   They were dressed in passing poor taste too."

"Ah," cried the wife, "'twas but a rich merchant who thought to leave for his native city of Leipsic to-day, and who wanted to see your prints.   I showed them to the fellow, and told him of their worth, but he took none."

Albrecht Dürer frowned slightly.

"Why did you not call me, as is usual?"

"Albrecht, you know how many times you have told

me not to announce a visitor to you unless you were
ready with fine dress and curled locks. And that you
were not this morning."

"'Tis true enough, wife, and you did well not to call,
especially since he took none."

Elsa dressed, after dinner, with great care. She
smoothed her skirt down stiffly, patted her red pointed
shoes softly, and braided her hair with silver threads.
For was not this a Holyday? And was not Werner
going to sing? And now she was ready, with her new
mantle about her.

Placing her feet carefully and with dignity on each
step the girl, holding her excitement under a sedate
manner, walked down the stairs and entered the front
room. Frau Agnes waited there with the master, and
the journeymen were coming in noisily. But the
mistress was no longer pleased. She had turned, like
a crock of cream, from sweet to sour, and she looked
as if crossing her ever so slightly would blast her disposition for the day. She held a pitcher in her hand.

Elsa stood perfectly still. Her face grew white as
linen. She was too fearful to speak. Frau Agnes
turned to her crossly,

"What means this? You have not completed your
work in the house for the day. I told you to finish
cleaning this pewter. And that you have not done."

Herr Dürer turned and frowned.

"Wife," he murmured, "let the maid do this on the
morrow. She has not time to-day. We must go now
to the church."

Frau Agnes drew her lips together tightly. Her headdress shook with sudden rage.

"Nay, such things she must do when the proper time comes. That I say. Go to your room and take off these gewgaws. Come, Albrecht." She wheeled heavily and went from the house. Herr Dürer, his face distressed, followed his wife, and the youths, looking subdued in clean blue blouses and red trousers, brought up the end of the procession. But Conrad left them and came to Elsa.

"Then will I stay with you, maid, and help you."

"Nay, Conrad, go with them," she answered chokingly, "for I mind not . . . much."

An apprentice appeared in the doorway, his small face unnaturally clean and his clothes unspotted with ink.

"Master says to come on, Conrad, and make haste about it." He disappeared.

"Go, Conrad," said Elsa sadly, "why should two of us miss the contest? There be nought to do, very much, here."

"Nay, 'twas just that the sour frau was angry with our master, and took it out on you. The Devil be pinching her to-day, methinks."

"Go on now, Conrad, for we wish not to offend Master Dürer. He wants all of his journeymen with him."

The boy turned sadly toward the door.

"Elsa, I like it not, leaving ye. This will be a dreary day for me now."

The girl smiled at him, as she slowly untied her mantle. But when he was gone she dropped a few tears on the pewter she was scrubbing. Fräulein Bach looked at her solemnly. Elsa stared at her a moment.

"Fräulein, for long I have wanted to hear Werner in the contest. Why should I miss it now? 'Twill take not long to clean this pewter, for most of it I did yesterday. If I go, think ye they will see me in such a crowd?" Her eyes brightened and she hastily went to work.

Elsa ran down Zisselstrasse. Looking around uneasily for fear she might see her mistress, the maid hurried to the bake shop and stared into its small panes. No, there was nobody within.

She walked to the public square, which was thronged. Bears and apes were performing on street corners, surrounded by country folk, and Elsa saw at one side of the market place the three famous Nürnberg cannons, called the Fishermaid, the Falcon and the Owl. Strung above her head by a rope from St. Sebaldus Church to the Town Hall was the shield of the Meistersingers. She stared at the picture painted on the shield. There were twelve stiff men cultivating a beautiful garden, which was threatened by a wild beast, who was creeping upon them, undiscovered by the men.

The whole town was gay. Elsa walked about, and was glad that she had come. She looked up at the clock on the Church of Our Lady. It was time to go to the contest, for already the clock figures were mov-

ing. She watched, fascinated, to see the procession
of trumpeters, electors and knights pass in front of
the throne of the Emperor Charles, who sat with his
eyes fixed woodenly on them. The electors doffed
their ermine caps stiffly. The trumpeters placed their
horns to their mouths, and when they had moved
slowly back into the dark works of the clock a figure
of Death came out and struck the hour with his
scythe. Boom! Boom! Boom! Elsa read, a little
frightened, the inscription on the big clock, "Man,
Remember Thy End."

The crowd was pouring now across the bridge of the
Pegnitz to St. Catherine's Church, and so the girl fell
in with it. All conversation was of the contest, and
she heard arguments all about her.

"The master's crown of laurel will go this day to
Hans Sachs, our cobbler poet, for he is king of them
all."

"Nay, not so. Sachs cannot make the beautiful
verses that his old teacher, Nunnenbeck, is master of.
The old, not the young, will win this day."

Elsa turned to look at the mob streaming into the
church. Feathers and ribbons and fur-trimmed robes!
There was a lilt to the atmosphere. As the folk
crowded into St. Catherine's each of them must drop
a coin into the hat of the sacristan, who stood, beaming, by the doorway. This was drink-money for the
man, and the custom was planned, it was said, to keep
out the poor and the beggars. "Ah," thought Elsa,
getting a coin from her small bag, "why should I enter

with the rich when but five short months agone they would never have let me in here? 'Tis but a change of costume."

There were songs and shouts from the street as she went into the chilly church, but she heard no master songs from outside, for it was considered profane to sing them save in the church. There were no seats vacant.

Elsa stood a moment and then she felt a large hand draw her to one side. It was Hans. She was dumb with amazement, for never before had she seen either Hans or Melchior, who stood beside him, in such clothes. They were gaudy as parrots, and Hans grinned proudly as he saw her surprise. He whispered:

"Maid, why are ye not with your household, down there near Master Pirkheimer?"

The girl saw, where he pointed, the long curls of Dürer resting on his velvet shoulders, and near him were the round cut head of Pirkheimer, the white starched linen of Frau Agnes' top wings, and the cropped hair of the row of journeymen. The two apprentices were too small to be seen through the crowd.

"She would not let me come, so I slipped away."

Hans laughed.

"'Tis well. That will serve her right. The woman be sour enough to make all the town's vinegar, for 'tis fatal to the stuff to make it with a sweet countenance."

Whispering ceased. Immense silence closed down

upon the packed church, as the Master Singers filed in and took their places.   They were dressed in silk suits of solid colors, some in black, some in green, blue, crimson or saffron, but all wore about their necks pleated lace collars and caps on their heads, and all carried on their faces important serious expressions. Could that be?   Surely not!   Yea, it must be Werner alongside Hans Sachs, whose hands still showed traces of his grimy occupation in spite of extra scrubbing. Ah, that Sachs had a lively eye!

Werner wore a tight suit of green velvet, which fit him so closely that he resembled a solemn frog.   Indeed he was unnaturally solemn.   Elsa had difficulty in recognizing him, while Hans next to her almost laughed aloud.

Elsa gazed proudly at their green friend, who looked, certainly, as important as did all the others.   No one else could sing such jolly verses as did Werner, with his carved cither in hand.   But look as she might, still she could not see any cither.   Oh well, she thought, perhaps he had it behind his bench.   She trembled excitedly as she thought of Werner and the prize. He would make them all laugh, and applaud when he began to sing one of his funny songs.   She could hardly wait to hear him.   It had been so long since his deep voice had startled the birds of the woods and fields, and had taken Elsa's troubled thoughts from herself.

Under a purple velvet canopy on the platform was the singer's stool, and back of it were placed, precisely, three tapestried judge's chairs.   Two black velvet curtains were looped before these chairs, to hide them and their slates, on which the judges jotted the number of mistakes. The dignitaries seated themselves, and the curtain was dropped solemnly in front of them.

The first contestant was a long fellow in crimson, who sang dully, exactly, and at great length many verses which made Elsa a little drowsy. She thought, gleefully, of how the place would wake up when Werner came up to enliven them with his song. But it was rather odd; the crimson fellow looked pleased with himself at the conclusion of his verses, and seemed to think that he had done well. Elsa stared at him contemptuously.

"Hark," whispered Melchior loudly, "methinks I know that fellow! He be the tooter who wakes the town wall gate-keepers every night. 'Tis thus he gets his long wind."

The next man stalked to the platform and seated himself nervously on the singing stool. But Elsa hardly noticed his song, for it was not only tiresomely stiff and solemn, but she could also hear the fat woman who stood next to her whispering his mistakes to her companion.

"In faith, he has already made the Blind Fault, the False-Flower Fault and the Clip-syllable Fault." And, no wonder that he did not succeed! Anything so wearisome could surely not win the prize. Evidently Hans Sachs was not singing to-day. Why did these townsmen sing as badly as that, she wondered?

At last, when she was so sleepy and tired that she was almost sorry that she had come, the girl saw a pudgy green form bounce onto the platform and seat itself. She stared and stared. Could this be Werner? He had a face as solemn and serious and sad as an owl. His very ears looked as if the weight of the world hung on them, as pieces of glass pull down the ears of gypsies. What could have happened to him she wondered, appalled?

He was singing. Elsa could scarcely move, so surprised was she. He was singing in measured cadence, serious verses, as dull and tiresome as the others had been, and he was sending them out across the vault of the packed building as if he had never, in all the days of his life, given vent to a burst of wild music on a hillside. Elsa clasped her hands in dismay.

"Hans," she cried, "what means this? Our Werner to sing this way?"

The big man smiled down at her, although he too looked a bit astonished.

"Yea, maid, this is the way Meistersingers sing. They do nothing save by rote and rule. Methinks Werner takes not long in learning to harnass his song in golden chains."

"Welladay!" murmured the girl, "I like it not. But, it is much better, even so, than the others sang, and I doubt not he will win the crown."

Melchior cocked one eyebrow at her.

"Of a certainty he will win it, for this song be more

deadly dull than all the others, and that is what they like."

The fat woman was displaying her knowledge of the rules again.

"'Tis the Barking Tone he did not give as he should. Can he manage the Straw-Blade, the Crimson and the Note-paper Tones?"

Elsa glared at her, sick with disappointment. But she resented the slurs cast on this song, for Werner was singing as precisely as anyone could wish. The voice of that woman grated on her ear.

"There! He has made mistakes in the Departed Gluttons Measure, the Cupids Hand Measure and the Hedge Blossom Measure. 'Tis six, and one more will cast him out of a chance at Master's Rank."

Werner finished his song, bowed low to the Meistersingers and went down into the audience.

"Ah," murmured the neighbor, "he ruined the Skylark, the Rosebud and the Bright Shining Thread tones!"

The judges came slowly from behind their curtain, and, with solemn words, bade the winner step up. It was on the head of the crimson man that they set a crown of laurel, and around his neck that they drew a golden chain embellished with the head of King David.

Hans looked sorrowfully down at Elsa.

"Maid, 'tis too bad. Our Werner was by far the best of the lot. I be sorry ye were disappointed so."

But Elsa's face was beaming.   She grinned delight-
edly at her kinsman, and cried,

"Ah, Hans, I care not for that.   I be terribly glad
that our Werner did not get it, for an he had he might
soon become as dull as that townsman in crimson."

Melchior twisted his mouth into a smile,

"Maid, those are the only sensible words I have heard
ye say since ye entered that nesting place of sharp
tongues and clean kerchiefs."

CHAPTER XI

THE WIND BLOWS COLD

THE boy bent over his table, absorbed in the small block of wood which he held in his left hand. The girl sat on a stool near-by, feet drawn up on the topmost rung, hands clutching the sides of her stool, her eyes watching quietly the tiny curled slivers of wood which fled before the small keen edge of the knife. It seemed remarkable to her that a picture of trees and houses and a figure of a man could be coming from that piece of carved wood. The big cluttered room was deserted save for these two.

Presently Conrad put down his work and went to the big portfolio cabinet at one side. He took out an armful, and turned to his companion with shining eyes.

"Elsa," he whispered, "come over here. Wouldst like to see these prints of our master's work?"

"Yea, Conrad," said the girl, "but will he not be angry an he catches us at it?"

"I think not, but he will not catch us at it. He is below stairs somewhere."

Two heads bent over the big portfolios, and two pairs of eager eyes looked and looked at the pictures.

"Do but see," cried Elsa, as she gazed at a drawing of a rabbit, "is it not wonderful? Every hair be put in as if 'twere the animal himself."

"Yea," said Conrad slowly, "but 'tis not that reason —though that be skill too—which makes the picture wonderful."

The girl looked puzzled.

"'Tis because," continued the boy, "he possesses such cleverness with mechanical details, and besides he gets a remarkable, unified effect."

"Nay, I know not what ye mean," said Elsa sulkily, "those be but words to make me wonder."

Conrad's face grew red with an unaccustomed effort to explain himself clearly.

"Welladay! I know not what to say, but he so carefully plans details—small things—blends . . . so as to give a picture of a whole . . . one complete picture, your eyes see . . . not confused by looking at many small details. But you see the whole thing as one." Conrad paused, looking baffled at his inability to express his thoughts.

"Ah," cried Elsa, "'tis like a seed cake. Ye look not at each seed, though ye know they are there on top; ye just look at the cake as a fine cake."

"Yea," laughed Conrad, "'tis somewhat of the same

idea." He turned a picture over carefully, and gave a low cry as he saw it.

"What?" murmured Elsa, anxiously. Conrad's face seemed so strange.

She looked again. It was the same picture of a big white horse which they had seen in a window on their first day in Nürnberg. She gasped. Conrad was speechless, and then his words broke from him with a rush.

"'Tis the same . . . the same. 'Twas that print I saw at my goldsmith master's . . . told him 'twas wonderful to do that. He spoke but of goldsmithry, so I left to seek a way . . . knew not Master Dürer . . . so he be the master after all."

There was a sound in the doorway. Conrad hastily shut the portfolio and raised his eyes fearfully. The artist was standing there, his look intent on the two. Conrad moved back to his table, while Elsa stood on one foot and then on the other, uncomfortably.

Dürer smiled a little.

"Conrad, look not so guilty. You have the privilege of seeing my works whenever you please."

The boy bowed jerkily.

"Lad, you work to-day, when all of my journeymen, and even the lazy 'prentices, have been given permission to attend the festival?"

Through the window Elsa caught a far-off strain of jolly music, and she heard eager feet running toward the center of town.

Conrad looked diffidently at his master.

"Master, I cared nought for festival doings.   I have taken part in many such, but I have not often before had a chance to do this work, which is not work either."

The artist's smile broadened.   He looked surprised and pleased.

"Boy," he said softly, "you are the only one of my young journeymen who says that.   They all rush from the house at my first word of permission.   You speak as I think, and as I was used to speak when a lad myself."

"You do like long hours, master?"

"Yea, I get so entangled in my work that I care not to leave off.   And stop but to eat and sleep oftentimes, as my good wife complains."

There was a thumping and bumping on the big street door.   It came to them with a hollow sound, traveling up the well of the staircase.   Elsa jumped as if she had been pricked with a needle, and ran from the door and down to answer the summons.   Master Dürer laughed.

"In faith the wife has the girl a-tremble."

Elsa was halfway down when she heard the great door open and the voice of Frau Agnes, first harsh, then honey-tipped.   "It must be a customer for Herr Dürer's work," thought the girl, as she bit her lip at the prospect of the tongue lashing she would receive for not being nearer the door when it was thumped. She ran on down, but stopped in the dark hall, timidly.

Inclosed in the doorway, outlined against bright sunlight, was a richly dressed gentleman.   Elsa stopped short, wondering what Frau Agnes would say. She knew, instinctively, that this must be the noble who had ordered the picture.

Frau Dürer bent low, as she asked the visitor in and bade him be seated until she could call her husband. Elsa moved quickly from the doorway and ran softly up to her room. She crouched on her high bed and listened. Every sound from below came to her, muffled. That was Frau Agnes speaking politely. Then the voice of the knight. Listen as she might she could not hear words, only sounds.

There were heavy footsteps coming part way up. That was the frau calling Herr Dürer. She heard his shoes as he walked down, answering the cry. His voice now made an undertone, deep and full, for the shrill echoes of his wife and the precise accents of the noble.

Elsa wanted badly to know what her mistress would say about the picture that had been made for the knight and was not there for him. But she could not hear. What would happen if Frau Agnes did not tell? And what should she, Elsa, do?

The front door opened. The man was leaving. His voice came through the house once more, and then his steps went out. She could hear Dürer and his wife arguing. The girl rose and went quietly down the stairs. Whom would the master suspect? She wondered if she should tell what she had seen.

The voices came from Herr Dürer's studio on the first floor. Elsa could only catch a few words, as she

went into the kitchen.   But she did not hear Frau
Agnes admitting anything.   She stopped in dismay.
What were they saying?

"Wife, where could it be?   Just last week I put that
panel here.   Important work, this commission."

"How should I know?   Perhaps one of these thieverly journeymen . . . what do we know of them—
especially the new one . . . vagabond and tramp.
Serves you well for taking a commission so cheaply."

"Nay, Agnes, it could not have been one of my journeymen.   I cannot believe save in Conrad's honesty.
'Tis strange.   The panel is gone completely."

Elsa caught a glimpse through the half-open door
of the master seated on a settle, with pictures stacked
all about him.   His elbows rested on his knees, and
his hands were in his yellow hair, twisting it out of its
usual order.   The girl stood appalled.   Never before
had she seen the master so worried that he allowed his
hair to become disarranged, for he had great pride in
its luxuriance, and would not leave his room of a
morning till it had been curled.   And his face was
drawn, etched with deep lines.   He looked older somehow, and very sad.

"When the boys return I shall call them all before
me.   We will sift this thing out."

Elsa tiptoed into the back of the kitchen and was
busy at the stove when her mistress, whose face was
strangely cold and quiet, came in to give her orders for
work of the next day.   The girl glanced quickly at
the woman, and then lowered her eyes.   Above her the

face was stiff and the eyes had a steely glitter.   Elsa
didn't want to see them again.

A sudden memory smote the girl.   She could see
again the dark studio, and the figure of her mistress,
by a feeble candlelight, taking a picture from the
cabinet.   She had wondered much, and more when
she saw Frau Agnes bowing away the gaudily dressed
merchant.   He had placed gold in her hand too.   Elsa's knees trembled.   And they might accuse Conrad!
She wondered desperately how she might prevent them
from accusing Conrad.   Only by telling what she
knew of Frau Agnes.   But she did not think that she
could do that to the master.

That day there was a strange air of desolation about
the big house beneath the castle wall.   It was quiet.
Dürer shut himself up in his studio, after a search of
the house.   Conrad, having helped him look, returned,
not much concerned, to his work above.   Frau Agnes
went starchily, saying little, as was not her way, and
with that stubborn, cold look in her eyes.   Elsa moved
about softly, pale and oppressed, trying to solve the
problem, in her mind, of what she should do.
"Surely," she thought, "she will not let anyone else
take the blame."   But even as she tried to reassure
herself she grew more distressed.

· That night she dreamed that Conrad was in the
deep well of the near-by castle, and she was trying to
pull him up in a bucket, but every time she got the
bucket to the top, with a tremendous effort, she found
that Fräulein Bach was in it, and that Conrad was still

below, calling to her that he was drowning. Behind her she saw Frau Agnes, who had turned, mysteriously, into a great wild boar, with antlers on her head and corals and shells about her neck, coming to devour them. All about she could smell the faint odor of starch, which was a complete part of her mistress always.

Elsa woke next worning more tired than when she went to bed, and she rose wearily.

As soon as the last sleepy apprentice had swallowed his thin slice of bread and butter, and had covered himself in his first layer of ink and paint, the master called the wondering boys together in the big front room below. Elsa came, standing quietly near the door, and Frau Agnes loomed, like a statue, behind her husband. Dürer looked inexpressibly tired and forlorn as he turned his head apologetically to look at his household. The boys ceased whispering, and stared back at him, with round inquiring eyes.

"Young masters, I accuse you all of nothing, for I do trust you completely. But I must ask you, all assembled, if you have seen aught of the painted panel, of a Madonna and Child, on which I spent so much time and thought and work this winter. It was a commission executed for a gentleman who lives far from here. He came for it yestreen, and I discovered its disappearance. I have promised it, and cannot deliver it."

The boys gazed at him in surprise. Not one of them looked guilty. Dürer stared at each one, and then smiled sadly. "I see that you know nought of this matter. You may go." But his wife stopped them.

"Stay, Albrecht! Where could it be?" The youths fingered their blouses, dumfounded. One little fellow smeared a spot of ink round and round on his chin with a grimy thumb until he looked as if he had been marked from infancy by the black man.

There came a loud thump on the door. Elsa jumped nervously. A servant entered and held open the door for his master who wore the purple garments of a learned knight.

"Ah, Herr Albrecht Dürer. I am come for the panel again, so anxious am I for it. You could not find it yesterday. No doubt it is ready now?"

His sharp nose was tilted high. He was quite composed, as if he thought that it really could not be true that his order should have been misplaced.

The master went forward to bow the guest into his house, while the wife curtsied and smiled, albeit a little fearfully. The journeymen shuffled their feet uncomfortably.

"My private chapel is finished, and the wall space is ready for the Madonna," announced the gentleman importantly.

The master's face was distressed. He spoke slowly, "I have nought but trouble to report to you. I spent many hours working on your panel, and gave it my best attention. Now, when I look in my cabinet, where I placed it carefully, it is gone. I know not where."

The visitor's brows drew together in a frown.   He compressed his lips.

"I remain in the city two days," he said, "send a messenger to the Inn of the Golden Rose when it be found."   The noble inclined his head and opened the door.   As he did so he stood a moment staring intently at two men who pushed past him.   Then the gentleman from Cologne stepped into his carriage and was driven away by his servant.

Elsa shuddered convulsively.   Conrad could scarcely believe his eyes.   When he had recognized the first of the two fellows who were in the doorway, he pushed the girl quickly behind him and remained rigidly waiting.   The fiery whiskers of Red Cock quivered as he turned his head around.   Dürer and his wife, too amazed to utter a sound, stared at the man.   He advanced two steps, and then moved to one side.   Elsa could not suppress a sob.

There was the dark, still figure of a man.   His long, somber robe hung from gaunt shoulders.   Elsa's eyes traveled up to his face, stern and set, eyes half shut. The master recovered from his astonishment, and bowed before his unexpected guest.

"Good sir," he asked, "what can be done for you in my house?"

But the harsh voice of the bowman interrupted, ringing out suddenly, as he pointed to Elsa.

"'Tis the maid."

The dark man turned his head quickly to Dürer.

"Who is that maid?"

"She is our servant.   We received her into the house four months agone.   And a very good maid she is." He smiled at her, but the girl could scarcely see him. Before her were the flaming eyes, burning into her consciousness.

"There be the witch!" cried Red Cock.

A series of small gasps ran from youth to youth. Dürer looked intently at the girl, and then, as if reassured that she could not be a witch, he spoke,

"Sir, I believe not that the maid can be a witch."

But the stranger answered,

"Herr Dürer, I have searched the town of Nürnberg for this witch-maid, and now have I found her!"

There was silence.

"What means this assembly?" asked the man.

The master spoke coldly:

"A small private matter.   A painting of Madonna and Child, which a noble ordered, has disappeared. We know not where?"

"Disappeared!   Ye know not where?"

The witch-hunter straightened.   His brows came together.   He pointed at the girl.

"'Tis the witch.   How else could it disappear? She must have spirited it away, from malice to ye all.   Does this girl have an evil black cat with her?"

"Yea, she has a black cat, the Fräulein, and this panel is the one in which I painted into the background the cat."

"Ah," cried the stranger, "could ye have more proof?   Think ye the witch could want more than

to spirit away a pious picture. And she did it by
getting ye, all unknowing, to put in the likeness of
the evil instrument of Satan."

"Nay, that I did not," whispered Elsa. But the
room was in a confused welter of sound. Only Frau
Agnes, strangely, said nothing.

Conrad's face was crimson with rage, and Herr
Dürer looked at the stranger in horror. Elsa's gaze
remained a moment on the face of Frau Agnes, who
was stiff and silent. She dropped her eyes as the girl
looked at her.

Red Cock, with his whiskers jutting aggressively, led
Elsa through the door into the sunlit street. She
went slowly and quietly.

The girl could hear the youths whispering, excited
and sibilant, behind her, and the gentle voice of Herr
Dürer, compassionately telling Conrad that he need
not worry for he would get, immediately, Wilibald
Pirkheimer, the foremost rich man of the town, to
help them clear the maid. But the girl felt no hope,
only a dull ache because she must leave this house.

Down the street they went, a strange trio. Once
more Elsa saw the wide black robe swaying beside
her, but her heart was a lump of lead now.

The streets were filled with a hoydenish crew. In
so much confusion the three were scarcely noticed.
Stages were being erected at some corners in the
streets, and around these were crowds, many folk
wearing huge contorted heads of strange animals made
of cloth on their shoulders.

On rough stages were plays. Little boys dressed as

angels sang, while comedians, with coarse humor, ridiculed Judas, who was, indeed, a comic character.   And they made merry in the guise of grave watchers, cowardly braggarts, dealers in spices to the three Marys, quacksalvers, thieves and quarrelsome wives.

Elsa and her two companions, who kept a tight clutch on her arms, were pushed and hauled about roughly by the laughing mob, and were often forced to halt.   But there was little mirth for the girl, who saw in the stage flames, which rose in red rags, real fires, mounting upward around a stake, and the comic chatter of the merry imps was to her but the crying of a mob.

Through the market place they passed to the Town Hall, and that passage was a torment to the girl.   How quickly a merry crowd can become a howling mob, thirsting for its victim, she knew.

Elsa was thankful that her three friends, and Conrad, were not caught in her net, and she hoped fervently that they would not endanger their lives by trying to help her.   She thought that there was no aid possible now.

They reached the Town Hall, where Grumchen went to seek the Clerk, whom he could not find because the fellow was celebrating the festival in the streets, or in some wine cellar.

"Where is the jailer?" asked the witch-hunter sternly of a pompous little clerk.

"Sir, he is not here this day, for we have uncommonly few prisoners in the Loch, only some harmless beggars, and I, I alone, be in charge."

The dark man drew his brows down suddenly.

"Is this the way to keep a Town Hall? The girl is a witch, and must be placed in dungeons before she can do evil to the city. To-morrow will be the trial."

"Here, here are the keys. Let your soldier take her," muttered the clerk apprehensively. "Mayhap your bowman had better stay to guard her."

Red Cock thought longingly of the wine cellar, and revelry. He grumbled:

"Sir Master, how can the maid, for all she be a witch, get from the Loch dungeons?"

"Yea, there is no need to guard her, and she be placed there securely." Then, to the clerk, "Keep the keys safely, and give them not into any hand till I come again, or this witch will fell ye with a fateful malady."

The little clerk trembled mightily, but he swelled his chest.

"Nay, sir, nobody in this whole city would dare take them from me. I be the first assistant clerk."

"Do ye, Red Cock, stay on the steps of the building until I return." The bowman nodded, and disappeared with the girl, but, he thought as he went, "there is a cellar near-by, and that is close enough to keep watch from."

Elsa was roughly thrust down a dark, damp stone stairway and into a room where one tiny ray of light filtered through cobwebs into her gloom through a slit in the solid walls. She lay on the cold floor, and heard the heavy door swing to behind her, and fasten with a groan of rusty hinges.

Chapter XII

THE END MUST BE

WHEN the great door of the artist's house slammed shut behind Elsa, Conrad stood with his eyes fixed on the wall, scarcely able to realize the sudden change which had taken place. Around him the boys shuffled their clumsy feet, and nudged each other, whispering excitedly. Frau Agnes turned with a whirl of her wide skirts and boxed an apprentice on his ears, for no reason at all that the little boy could see. She hurried from the room, leaving the victim of her anger grimily wiping away his tears.

Herr Dürer, his eyes troubled and his chin resolutely set, searched rapidly for his cloak and cap. He hastened into the street, calling back as he went,

"Boys, get to your work as soon as might be. I go to see friend Pirkheimer, and so will not be with you at all to-day."

The youths trouped upstairs, talking louder now,
and laughing.

Still Conrad stood, knowing neither what to do, nor
how to do it.   He only knew that he must do something.   Then he remembered Hans, kinsman of Elsa.
Hans must know at once.   The boy rushed into chilly
streets, oblivious of the cold and of his lack of cap or
coat.

The mob of joyful maniacs only enraged him, for it
shouted, yelled, sang and danced wildly.   He had great
difficulty making his way to the small uphill street
on which he knew Hans' bakeshop perched.   And if
the big man should not be there, but should be at the
carnival?   Well, in that case there would be nothing
to do but look for him, if the city itself had to be
combed.

The youth pushed and shoved his way resolutely
through the crowd, until he emerged on the little side
thoroughfare.   The passage was dark under overhanging eaves of houses.   The door of the small shop was
shuttered tightly, and Conrad could see nothing
through the tiny window save empty shelves.   He
sighed in despair, and turned to the festive market
place.   There was little more hope of finding anyone
there, with folk in mask and clown heads, than there
would be in looking for a lost purse in a gypsy camp.

Conrad was suddenly grasped by many hands and
forced to dance about in a circle, while his captors
capered and roared lustily.   The youth glared help-
lessly, then on the second time round he doubled his

fists and let fly in the faces of two of his tormentors, on one side and then the other.   As he ran he turned and saw them sitting in the mud, too astonished and befuddled to swear.

In the market place was a dancing, yelling throng. The youth stood, dazed a moment, and then gave a cry of joy.   Luck was with him!   Standing in the front ranks of a group was the baker, big arms folded across a massive chest.   He glared, and from deep in his throat came a hoarse disgusted rumbling, breaking ever so often into speech.   Facing him, the center of attraction, were two dirty little musicians, cither and zinck in hand.

"Hum-m-mm!   Ye think ye play, do you?   'Tis nought but the squealing of pigs.   Ye think ye play, do you?   Yon zinck calls forth the sounds of a mother cow looking for her calf.   Werner could draw music from that cither, but, ye dolt, ye disgrace the name of musician."   He wheeled.

"Ha!   Conrad, 'tis the Fiend's own music, if it can be called by the name."   He stared at the youth's face, then drew him to a quieter space in the shadow of a house.   "What brings the frown?   Has aught happened to the maid?"

"Yea, and that right badly.   Our good master— a picture was lost he had made . . . much work . . . for a noble.   Found picture gone and Red Cock came just then . . . Grumchen too . . . one as venemous and tother as braggart as ever!   They accused her of witchcraft—of spiriting the picture away . . . took

her to Town Hall Loch instantly.   Our master has
gone to consult Wilibald Pirkheimer."   He gasped
out the words.

Hans eyes took on that glassy staring surface, which
Conrad knew from experience meant that the big man
was thinking hard and furiously.   His hands clenched,
and his throat began to rumble again, inarticulately.
Conrad waited.   Hans drew the boy into a dark side
street.

"Friend," he said softly, "we must look for Werner
and Melchior, and make a plan to get her away from
prison.   If we can but reach the monastery on the
road from the Spittlerthor we find safety, for 'tis
gainst Nürnberg law to take a runaway from that
place."

Conrad's face grew white and drawn.   He dug his
fingers into his palms.   His eyes were miserable.
Then he sat down quietly on a doorstep and dropped
his head in his hands.   Hans said nothing.   He
seemed not to notice the boy, for the idea beginning
to take shape in his round head was requiring all of
his attention.

But Conrad could see only the two things.   He had
come to a place where he must make a decision which
would influence his whole future.   Beyond their
small shelter he could hear the sounds of revelry, horns,
voices, songs, music.   To go away meant giving up his
work here with his master.   It meant scanty food,
cold nights, no opportunity to ever learn to be the
artist he was beginning to believe that he might be-

come.   He knew that he was considered by the master
to be one of the most promising journeymen.   In a
few years he could make his masterwork, a painting,
or a set of prints in wood or metal, and the success of
that would mean that he could take his wanderyear,
studying in Holland under great masters, and in Italy,
that marvelous world of art.   And when he returned
to Nürnberg he could set up his own studio.   Conrad's eyes glowed with the fire of his thoughts.

But he thought of the maid.   He plunged his hands
into his long hair and closed his eyes.   Hans turned
and looked at him.

"Lad," he said quietly, "ye need not go.   Three of
us are stout enough.   An I were your age, and had
your gift, so would not I give it up neither."

"Nay," cried the boy, leaping to his feet.   "I am
with ye all, Hans.   Let us go at once . . . find the
others."

Plunging back into the crowd they made their way
as fast as was possible to the cobbler's shop of Hans
Sachs, where Werner was wont to sing and tap.   Under a linden tree they saw the small house peering at
them through two little windows.   Hans pushed the
door, and entered hurriedly.   There was a pungent
smell of leather and oils, mixed with equally pungent
sounds of song and the rap of tools.

Werner sat on a stool, working and singing lustily,
and on the other side of the room was his master, who
added a verse to the other's song when the fat little
man paused for breath.   Roared Werner:

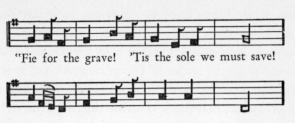

"Fie for the grave! 'Tis the sole we must save!

So sayeth the priest and the cobbler.   Ha!"

He bounced to his feet, and reached up to pound his friends' shoulders.

"Ha! Glad I am to see ye both! But why the solemn faces? 'Tis a festive day. I must stay within and finish this job till sundown, by order of yon tyrant." He waved his hand toward Hans Sachs, who came forward, wiping grimy fists on his leather apron and grinning amiably.

Hans grasped his little friend's arm firmly.

"Werner, the man possessed of demons has arrived here, and discovered our maid at Master Dürer's house. He even accuses her of spiriting away a picture. But now she be in the Town Hall jail. 'Tis up to us to take her from there. What say ye?"

The fat man opened his mouth wide in astonishment. Then he closed it with a snap.

"What say I? Why I say, may all the Foul Fiends take the man! What say I? May the brimstone flames devour him! What say I? Why, I say get ye from that door! We go at once."

"Stay!" called Sachs. "What be this trouble?"

Conrad explained hurriedly, and somewhat confusedly, while Hans tried to calm the little fat man sufficiently to allow the words to be understood.

"Come," said Sachs, "there is a secret passage from the Loch dungeons under to the graveyard, for it was dug but last year to lay a pipe for water. Mayhap ye might get her out through that, by digging yourselves through the cemetery?"

"We be more likely to dig ourselves into the graveyard than out of it!" cried Werner.

"But I have a plan," boomed Hans. "Hear it first. Sit ye all down."

They pulled up benches to sit soberly and hear what Hans had to say, although Werner was useless, since he could not stay in one spot long enough to talk, but bounced up and down the long room shaking his fists.

"First," said Sachs, when Hans had finished, "I will tell ye all that there might be a chance of success in this wild venture, for Splengler, the Town Clerk, and all of the other officials are not in office to-day. Only a little assistant be in charge. 'Twould be strange if ye could not outwit him. But I like not the thought of losing my helper here," he finished ruefully, "for he can sing passing well, though he be but an indifferent cobbler."

Werner stopped to turn his wrath explosively on Sachs.

"An what are ye, if not a poor workman, when ye spend more time on poetry than on leather. Beshrew me, but I can beat ye any day at either."

Sachs grinned as Werner snapped his fingers contemptuously, tore his apron from his waist and plunged into the house, emerging presently with his cither clasped lovingly under his arm.

"Farewell, friend," he cried to his master, "an there be one house in the world could tame my roving spirits, this be the place."

Hastening to the bakeshop Hans came out in his old clothes, looking more natural without baker's white, and with his zinck swung around his neck in old-time manner. They hurried to the inn where Melchior was last seen by them, but the inn-keeper said he was not on the premises. Nothing for it then but to look for him in the town. They scattered, agreeing to meet in an hour's time before the door of St. Lorenz Church. Conrad went, with a sick heart, to help ferret out the tall fellow.

After a fruitless search he decided that it must be an hour since he had parted from his two friends, and perhaps one of them had already found Melchior. He turned to retrace his steps toward the church, but was forced to halt on the side of the street to let a long procession go by.

There was a line of men, all clad in flowing white cloaks and tall white caps, marching solemnly toward the chilly River Pegnitz, where the bathhouses, which perched gayly on the banks, were ready to receive the first visitors of the year.

At the tail of the procession walked a tall lank figure, wrapped in the voluminous white cloak which Nürnbergers wore to the bath. Conrad stared amazedly, then plunged forward and grasped him by the arm.

"Melchior, what art doing here?"

"Touch me not," quoth the fellow with dignity, "for I be going to the bathhouse, where, in addition to washing, we get fine food and fine conversation."

"Come with me," begged the youth.

"Nay, nay. I go to the bath. 'Tis the sleepiest occupation ever I saw yet, and 'tis this pleasing life which may yet keep me in Nürnberg."

"But Melchior," cried Conrad, following the procession and trying to retain a hold on the fellow's arm, "but Melchior, the maid . . . taken to a dungeon . . . Hans and Werner . . . looking for ye . . . must come." He stammered excitedly.

Melchior sighed gustily, "Zounds! I but find me a choice life to lead when someone snatches it from me." But he turned, his face long and sad, and went with Conrad to the church.

There they found Hans impassively waiting, and Werner, growing impatient. Melchior sighed again, prodigiously, took off his cloak and cap, folded them regretfully, and handed them to a passing youth.

"Take these," he said, "they be no use to me now."

In the Town Hall the fidgety little clerk sat on his stool figuring industriously, and trying not to listen to the strains of jolly music filtering into the gloom of his office. His rabbit nose quivered sensitively as his pen moved. There was a hearty shout at the door, and the voice of a cither broke the quiet of his corner. He was offended by the vulgar noise.

"Get ye from my room!   What do ye here?"

Four queer figures bounded into his seclusion and he stared in amazement at them.   One, he who twanged the cither noisily, was dressed in faded green, with a dilapidated cloak billowing behind him.   On his shoulders rested the monstrous head of a wild boar, teeth extended.

The second fellow, tall and lank, capered like a grass cricket under a false face, horribly painted.   The third, a big, heavy creature, pounded his feet on the floor, and the voice which issued from a stag's head, with branching antlers, rumbled frighteningly.   The fourth reveler was slim; he wore a red devil's suit, with dangling tail, and the crimson head, with staring eyes and horns above, sent cold chills down the spine of the amazed clerk.

"Get ye out.   Out!   Out!"

But they cavorted and yelled, and grasped him, with no respect for his dignity, pulling him into the center of the room.   They danced about him, and as they shouted one of them would pluck some of his personal possessions from him.

"A clerk went a-reveling, out he hied,
　　Oho!   Oho!   Oho!
　　He lost his keys from off his side,
　　Oho!   Oho!   Oho!"

Off came the weighty bunch of keys and disappeared behind the singer.

"May the Black Fellow take ye," shrilled the agonized clerk, clutching at the air. "Ye be drunk, the lot of ye, and ye will all spend the night in jail."

> "Said he, this coat cannot be,
>   Oho! Oho! Oho!
> It ill befits a blade like me,
>   Oho! Oho! Oho!"

Off came his coat, and was flung behind a settle.

> "And now, said he, 'tis time to choose,
>   Oho! Oho! Oho!
> Dancing feet or a clerk's old shoes,
>   Oho! Oho! Oho!"

Down came the shrieking clerk, whose noise could not be heard outside, in that din, and off came, not only his shoes, but all of his sober outer clothes. Tears of rage stood in his eyes, but his dignity almost succumbed under the shock when there he was in the devil's suit and head, and the slim youth emerged in journeymen's garb, which he had worn beneath carnival dress.

The clerk sobbed and yelled, as he was borne by force out of the door, and into the mob, where two of his captors kept a tight hold on each arm, as they shouted and danced.

The youth, seizing the huge bunch of keys, dashed through the passageway into the depths of the build-

ing.   He did not know his way around, and so he ran
through the many fine rooms, seeking the door to the
Loch.   His footsteps echoed in the empty place, but
he did not stop for breath until he plunged into the big
hall, where he saw, suddenly, on either wall, two immense paintings, pictures of Emperor Max surrounded
by his courtiers.   Conrad's feet paused, automatically.
He looked and looked, and then, with a sob, he fled
from the room.

At last he reached the prison door.   As it opened
protestingly the youth was almost overpowered by
the damp, moldering smell of the place.   And Elsa
was here!   All thought of anything but her safety
left him.   He ran, his feet making hollow sounds on
the stones, calling and crying her name.   There was
a faint answer down a crooked passage.   He dashed
into it.

As if in a daze the girl rose from the cold floor and
allowed the youth to pull her rapidly through the door
and upstairs.   He dashed by the big hall as if the fiends
were after him.   The girl blinked at the bright light of
the street.   The world was a vast caldron, boiling
furiously.

CHAPTER XIII

CROW OF THE COCK

THREE mad revelers, who held a devil in their midst, cavorted and danced through the crowd. Carnival spirit was high in Nürnberg town, for was not to-morrow the first day of Lent, when all must fast and pray?

Truly the mob was a wild one; yet the maddest of the lot was a certain small devil who made the day hideous with his shouts.

"Cut not so gay a caper, friend Imp," cried the Boar's Head as it bobbed alongside. "'Tis fitting to celebrate, but why be so frenzied?"

In truth the devil was a mad one, for he shrieked, he yelled, he danced, he shook. The Boar's Head and False Face held him with firm hands, but had difficulty doing so. He clutched at nothing, and uttered strange sounds, until folk around him noticed his antics, and one remarked,

"In faith, the fellow must be a walking barrel of wine?" Whereupon Stag nodded his great head slyly, as he answered,

"Yea, we be trying to keep him in check, for we did promise his mother to look out for him to-day."

Dusk was closing in upon the frolic, lengthening strange shapes in shadows. Fires were flaming in the streets, and by the light of torches a play was commencing on the largest stage set up in the market place. The crowd was thick about it.

"We must rid ourselves of this idiot, and begone," whispered Stag to Boar. In answer Boar's Head nodded ponderously toward the stage.

Pushing and shoving roughly the four made their way to the first ranks of the audience, impatient to see their play, written by the chief gunmaker of the city, and performed as the crowning feature of the spring carnival each year. It was called Mirth and the Devil, and was bursting with coarse witticisms.

When the loud and boisterous newcomers arrived in the front ranks of the jostling throng they saw the end of a lively battle between a stern monk and a gay devil, who sent ripples of laughter through the crowd as he dodged incense clouds, curses, and crockery, which the zealous priest threw at him. But the father had him cornered at last, and the crowd roared encouragement.

"At him, Father!"

"Send him back to the Little Master, King Lucifer!"

"Give him a sore noddle!"

The devil trembled on the edge of the platform, and then suddenly disappeared, as a big hand caught him by the ankle and jerked him off.

"The Devil!   Where is the Imp?" roared the mob, deprived of its fun.

"Here," shouted a voice, "here is the Imp.   He can lead the Father a chase.   He is the most devilish Imp in Christiandom!"   A tall man in a stag's head lifted the wriggling imp to the stage, and pushed him toward the actor.

Laughter swept the crowd again, growing as it rolled, for, in truth, the imp was a merry and curious devil.   He was ten times livelier than before he fell. He jumped, and leaped, and shouted and shrieked, and each yell was punctuated with the sound of broken platters.

"'Tis a merry conceit!   He calls himself the first assistant clerk of the Town Hall.   Ah!   Ha!"

Sir Stag and False Face slipped quietly from the crowd, and made their way, dragging Boar's Head, who was so pleased with sight of the lively devil on the platform that he was loth to leave.

Reaching the gate in haste they saw with relief that the boy and girl were already there, crouching back into the shadow of the Gate Tower.

"Maid," whispered Hans, throwing off his antlers, "'tis glad we are that ye got here safely.   Come, we must out before the clerk be able to make anyone understand him, or before Red Cock discovers our absence."

"Ah, yea," the girl replied with a sigh, "'tis like ye all to give up your fine jobs for me. But the road calls not to me now. I will come."

She bowed her head sadly, and went with her friends through the gate, not daring to look back. But when they reached the road, and were leaving the city noise and waving torches behind them, Elsa stopped suddenly, and cried,

"Ah, cousin Hans, we have left my Fräulein, and who knows what will happen to her? They think she be the instrument of the Black One who caused that picture to disappear. I can go not without her."

The four halted in consternation.

"Maid, I clean forgot the lively Fräulein. Our company be not complete without her. I will go back and get her, and do ye four go on. I will meet ye at the Monastery," spoke Hans slowly.

"Nay, friend Hans," said Conrad nervously, "'tis my job. I'll go. Ye know not even how to get in house—they would not let ye . . . I know where . . . I'll meet ye all."

"'Tis so. He speaks truly," said Werner.

"But keep from that wife, who dwells within," murmured Melchior disgustedly, "for she be vicious as an adder."

Elsa saw him turn to go, then she clutched the lad by his arm.

"Nay, Conrad. Ye know how I think of my Fräulein Bach, but I cannot let ye go into danger like that for us."

"There be no danger for him, maid," spoke Hans kindly, "for Grumchen could not know that he be with us. Let him go. He can join us soon at the Monastery."

And so they parted, Conrad to go back along the road to the lights of the town, and the other four toward the forest.

"Ah, the wind feels keen to my face," exclaimed Werner, but the girl only looked at the rough road, and walked as if she were in a stupor.

Passing fields and lonely farmhouses, the travelers made their way as rapidly as they could walk, and every so often one of them looked back over his shoulder, but saw nothing save wavering shadows of trees and the long road stretching behind. A roadside tavern loomed sharply around one bend in the highway, but Hans, who moved forward to reconnoiter, reported that the place seemed too still and dark to be pleasant. It was probably one of the many inns frequented by bandits. The little party crept by quietly on the dark side of the road, but Elsa, looking fearfully across, saw a single light burning before one window. She breathed better when they had left the place safely behind.

They walked out of tree shadow into a track which wound through open fields. The moon was rising, flooding the country, outlining the travelers as they plodded along. Hans looked unconcerned and placid, but Werner became disturbed.

"Good Hans," he whispered, trying not to frighten

Elsa, "methinks we be visible for some distance here. 'Twould be wise, just for safety's sake, to cut us some good stout staves, since we have not weapons. I do feel more natural to have a weapon in one hand and a cither in the other, than to let the right fist swing free on a lonely road. Think ye not so?"

"Yea," answered the big man. "They have served to save our noddles by cracking open others many a time before this. But that we cannot do till we reach yonder wood, where stout staves grow."

There was a faint clop, clopping noise, growing louder. The musicians stared at each other in alarm, and Elsa looked up with scared eyes.

"Think ye they have caught Conrad?" she cried.

"Not so," replied Hans, "he be safely back in Nürnberg town. 'Tis the four of us in danger. Quick, into that field, and lie flat."

But already horses were pounding the rough road toward them, and men were shouting. There was no time to hide; they were already seen. Elsa dropped flat in the edge of the field of grain, as her friends tried to assume a nonchalant air.

"Who be ye, going there?" came a hoarse voice.

The horses drew up, snorting, before them. Their riders dismounted, and the girl saw them to be soldiers of the city of Nürnberg. She saw, also, a buff jerkin, and caught a glimpse of fiery whiskers.

"We be but poor wandering musicians, good sirs," Werner pulled his hat low over his face, and bowed, "on our way back from carnival doings in the city.

We have a long way to walk, and so must start early."

The four soldiers stared at him, and then, reassured, at his cither, and at the zinck and dudelsack of the other two. But Red Cock, his chin jutting aggressively, glared at them. Hans edged quietly around the side of the Rohte Hahn, while his friends each picked out with his eyes a man to attack, in case of necessity.

Red Cock strode forward and snatched the cap from Werner's head.

"Aha! I thought so. Beshrew me, but 'tis the same evil three. The witch must be close by. Seize them!"

Elsa raised her head. There was a wild yell as Melchior, with a bony hand, grasped two soldiers and knocked their heads resoundingly together. They cracked as they met like a nut shell under the heel of a vigorous woman. Elsa hid her pale face in her hands.

When she looked up again fearfully she saw Werner, who had leaped on the back of a tall fellow, choking him from behind, as the man lashed out wildly with his arms. Hans was rolling over in the road in the bear grasp of Red Cock, who was trying to reach his own weapon. The horses stamped and ran away a little distance.

Werner was choking his victim purple, Hans had a tight grip on the head of Red Cock, and was pushing it ferociously into the mud, Melchior was cracking two soldiers' heads together with loud noises; but there yet remained one fellow.   He drew his musket up and laid about him viciously, for he could not fire for fear of shooting his own comrades.   Melchior fell, stunned, to the road, and Hans was knocked over on one side, but little fat Werner was struggling so energetically with his soldier, all the while swearing strange, loud oaths, that the fellow hit his companion by mistake.   And it was only after a terrific tussle with the musician that the soldier could subdue his wriggles and truss him up with ropes.

Elsa emerged from the field.   Red Cock rose, rubbing his face with his arms, sputtering muddily.   He saw the girl, and grasped her roughly by the arm.

"Ah, ye would fly, would you?   You evil poppet! I'll see that ye get burned this time, and your three spitfires along with ye."

He ran for his horse, dragging the girl with him, and threw her on its back.   He shouted to the soldiers.

"Bring in those cutpurses with ye, and make haste. We'll get them in dungeon this night.   To-morrow they will each be shorter by a head."

Elsa drooped over the horse's neck.   Her thoughts had almost lost the power to compel her attention. She only felt a great sorrow that her friends must die with her, and a great relief that Conrad was not with them when they were caught.   There was no use in trying to get out again.

She passed swiftly the black shadows of peasant hovels, and of tall, gaunt trees, not yet in leaf.   She saw the dark inn push suddenly into her vision, still with its one lonely light in the window, and as suddenly disappear.   She felt the steady swift jolt of the horse's feet, and in her throat there was a dull and steady ache.

As the soldiers, shouting to the crowd to make way, galloped into town, and toward the Town Hall, Elsa glimpsed a tall slim youth, who strode along, with something small and black in his arms.   He jumped back as they rushed upon him, and Elsa saw that it was Conrad.

The youth stopped dead still and stared at Red Cock, holding Elsa before him, and at his three friends trussed up like fowls, tied behind soldiers.   He looked a moment, while the men were trying to push their horses through the mob, and then he turned back upon the way he had come and went up again toward Zisselstrasse.   Elsa breathed a little sigh of joy to see him go without making himself known to Red Cock.

As they threaded their way through the laughing mob the girl saw, although her eyes scarcely registered the picture, a shrieking little devil who was the center of a jubilant crowd.   She shuddered.

The soldiers drew up their horses before the Town Hall door, and, dismounting, searched for the clerk. He and his bunch of keys were still missing.   Red Cock swore with a practiced tongue.

"The shrimp has disappeared, and if I had not come to see if all was well these witch stealers could have gotten clean away.   We will have to guard them. Needs must an the Little Master commands."

Elsa was pushed roughly down the damp corridor, and back into her big stone room, where she fell again on the cold floor. Then she was glad to see that her three friends were shoved in with her. The huge door clanged shut, and she could hear Red Cock, still swearing, as he bade the men bolt the door. A great iron bar fell into place. One soldier sat on the bench outside, disgruntled at his lonely job, and there was the echo of boots disappearing into the noisy regions above. The upper door slammed, ushering in a heavy silence. No gleeful sounds of revelry penetrated; there was but a steady drip, drip of water in one corner of the shadowed vault.

Elsa ran to her three friends and strove to unloose their leather thongs, while they whispered directions to her. At last they could move. They rose and stretched their cramped limbs, and walked about a bit, but they were all too depressed to say much. Then Werner, clapping his hand to his head, cried softly,

"Stay, we may yet win loose. Has not Conrad still the keys?"

But Hans smiled sadly,

"Yea, but that will not loose us, for there be a heavy bar to the door, and a bowman sits beside it. Up above stairs the others wait, and will not leave this time you may be sure."

Werner sat down and placed his sore head in his hands. There was not a syllable of song.

CHAPTER XIV

NÜRNBERG'S HAND

THE pale dawn light, a lean ghost, crept down through the tiny window into a dusky cold dungeon room. It touched stealthily the sleeping face of a girl, who lay on a straw pile, covered by a blue cloak, and then approached softly the figures, and swollen faces, of two men who sat dejectedly, and wide awake, against the wall. A third long figure was stretched out, in shadow, snoring with a monotonous, buzzing sound.

There was a step, heavy yet not solid enough for the boot of a bowman, in the corridor. The sleepy fellow left off his snoring suddenly, and sat up. All three heads turned, as on a pivot, toward the door. The girl trembled in her sleep, as if she dreamed of monsters.

An iron bar was pushed back, groaning rustily. The soldier who drowsed outside the door awoke and grumbled, but rose to the bidding of the person who came. Elsa sat up with a jerk.

"Who is it, cousin Hans?"

"I know not, maid.   But be not afraid."

"Nay," whispered the girl, "I have given up all hope." Her face was pinched and white in the pale light.

There was a loud thump, and the door drew open with another protest. A tall woman entered, with a candle, gleaming fitfully, in her hand. It lighted a heavy, bony face, forbidding and severe.

Hans stepped in front of Elsa.

"What do ye with the maid?"

"An who be ye to ask?" answered the woman harshly, "but I'll tell, being a kind woman, as I am. I am to search her, to find if she carry on her person aught of evil charms."

The three musicians fell back dejectedly. For a time there was silence, when Elsa had gone, for none felt like speech, so low were they in spirit. Torture for the condemned was by no means an unusual proceeding, and even in the free city of Nürnberg, where everyone knew that punishment was more just than in other cities, terrible means were sometimes used to make criminals confess. The three friends dared not think of these means, and yet they could scarcely tear their minds from the thought.

The great hands of Hans clenched and unclenched until his knuckles were white. Werner mumbled and swore. And Melchior stared at the damp ceiling with

melancholy eyes.   An hour drew to a close.   Melchior
spoke, his voice echoing through the stone vault in
eerie fashion.

"Hans, what think ye they will do with her?"

Werner thrust his round face close to the long one
and wagged his head angrily.

"Dost admit ye are a dolt?   Don't ye dare say!"

"Yea," rumbled Hans uneasily.   "'Tis best not to say.
We can but wait."

When it seemed to them that eternities had passed,
at last the iron bar drew back once more to admit six
soldiers, who roughly prodded the prisoners.

"Get ye up those stairs!" growled one of them.

"And that right quickly will we do," answered Werner.   "Nothing could be worse than not knowing
what is happening."

They were tied again with thongs and led singly
through the corridor, and up, into a long room.   As
they came above ground their eyes blinked at the
bright sunlight.   Hans saw that it must be well past
noon.   But his anxiety prevented notice of the hunger
pang at his chest.

Werner twisted his neck around.

"Hans," his voice hissed across the place, "this is the
hall of the Town Council, where burghers hold forth.
Witch proceedings be always secret.   How come we
here?"

"Nay," rumbled the big man, "I can say not why.
But if we be present at trial I be glad."   His eyes were
a hard blue, cold, brittle, glassy.   His fingers moved

in and out, in and out of his palms, below the thongs which drew blood from his wrists. He stood in captured strength, immovable save for the working fingers. Six soldiers formed a wall behind.

The door opened. A pompous man, the Magistrate, who paced through the hall to his decorated chair upon the platform. A weighty group, the Council, and solemn. Werner bounced almost joyfully and clucked in his throat as he observed genial Herr Pirkheimer, who stepped in beside Herr Dürer. The rich man looked unconcerned, but the artist bore a deep frown of distress graved into his forehead.

Splengler, the Town Clerk, poised his pen daintily, and then, as the burghers conversed in low tones, fell to jotting verses on the back of his paper. There was the plopping of a horse's hooves on stones outside. The familiar resonant strokes of the city clock fell, unfamiliarly, into the atmosphere of the room. The sounds gathered into themselves all of the weight of time, stripped of its natural cloak of the usual.

The door opened again. Pinpoints of light came into the eyes of Hans as he saw the thin, blackclad figure of Grumchen. Melchior wrinkled his nose in disgust as he caught a whiff of starch, and fixed his gaze on the stiff form of Frau Dürer. She seated herself with a crackling of garments.

The door swung wide, and closed. Elsa was visible as her guard, the tall woman, thrust her in. She walked backwards, for that was the law, until she neared the judge's platform, where she turned slowly around and stood, swaying a little. Her head drooped, and she seemed unable to lift her heavy eyelids.

Red Cock, the last to enter, bristled his fiery whiskers before the door, as if he alone expected the whole group to charge at him.

Werner suddenly whispered in the ear of Hans:

"In faith, the public trial must be on intercession of Dürer and Pirkheimer, for 'tis uncommonly strange."

The Magistrate rose. His voice came, deep and hollow. Werner stared at the golden chain about his neck and the rich fur of his gown.

"Elsa Muller, if thou be a witch, I do conjure ye confess."

There was no answer.

The woman prodded Elsa with a finger.

"Nay," whispered the girl, so low that the sound was like a little breeze blowing across the big room, "I be not a witch, and never was."

"Then," spoke the Magistrate, "we will consider three things, her reputation, the statements of witnesses, and the evidence. Through the mercy of the Council she has not been tortured, but an we find her guilty in these things she will be put upon the rack, and with pain made to confess."

The words came to Elsa as through a wall, with a thick, muffled sound.

"Who accuses this maid?"

Grumchen rose and bowed servilely.

"I, your honor."

"What is your name?"

"Johann Grumchen, may't please you, sir."

"Whence came you, and what is your business?"

"I come from all lands, all cities. I go to each in my pious search for evil-doers. An where I find them I deliver them, through my deep knowledge of magic, to punishment. That be my duty, since I alone know the secrets of finding out witches, and how to confound them."

A series of small gasps sped across the room. The eyes of all the company were fixed on the dark man.

The voice of the Magistrate came ringing and clear:

"Wherefore have you pursued this girl through many months and many places?"

The spare black figure swayed forward a little, and the neck was twisted around. He fastened his gaze on the judge.

"Good and just Magistrate, I did this because I knew that the rich and fine city of Nürnberg would not be safe an such a devilish witch-girl abode here."

The Magistrate stared at him, then spoke again, sternly:

"Be there a witness here to speak against Elsa Muller?"

Red Cock thrust out his chest. His fiery beard wagged as he exploded angrily,

"Yea, yea, good masters. For I myself saw three times this witch fly by black magic, with these minions of Satan." He looked triumphantly at the three musicians. "Yea, she did, with her devilish black cat, overturn me in forest, and go up in a burst of brimstone fire.   And, through her smoke she let fly one of my own bolts to pin me to the ground." Melchior gazed at him in astonishment.

"Yea, yea, good masters, an the second time she did get carried up on a stick at the wedding of a noble lord, and when we sent a great dog after her, she had a small red imp, with a tail of fire, burn him on his nose."

Hans clenched his fists tightly.   Werner glared ferociously at Red Cock, but, catching the solemn eye of the Magistrate, he subsided suddenly.   Melchior looked at the room of respectable Councilmen, and a great fear of the Law filled him.

The harsh voice of the fiery bowman continued:

"An the third time, by her devilish arts she sent an evil spirit into an inn-keeper, causing him to go suddenly mad and attack me!"

Hans drew in his breath with a little hiss.   He saw the Councilmen nod solemnly at each other, as if convinced by the evidence against the maid.   He saw satisfaction on the face of Red Cock.   He saw the pen of the lightsome Town Clerk pause in its poetic gyrations, and, with great seriousness, write down the words of the soldier.   He saw the maid, standing as in a stupor, sway slightly on her feet.   He saw the heavy woman, upright as the body of the Law, and as confident of her duty.   He saw Frau Agnes stiffen her neck, as if to prevent herself from looking with any pity on her maid.   He saw the long face of Melchior

lengthen still more in fright, and the round countenance of Werner grow blank with fear.   He saw,
looming large before him, the pompous, serious face
of the Magistrate.   And he saw the profile of Grumchen, dark and venomous as the beak of a bird of prey.
Hans bowed his head in hopeless rage and sorrow.

There was silence a moment, a space of time as long
and black as the shadow of a gibbet in the moonlight.
Hans raised his head slowly and looked at the lean
figure of the witch-hunter as it stood, swinging its
doctor's robe.   The dark man raised his voice,

"Yea, Magistrate.   The maid be the daughter of
a witch, who was caught destroying crops, and doing
other evil deeds, in the Rhineland, and was burned, as
was right.   The witch-girl disappeared, and was received, how and by what dark means of sorcery I know
not, into the house of the master artist, Albrecht
Dürer.   I accuse her of witchcraft, and make plea
that she be burned as an evil one, or cast to beasts."
He sat down.

Hans' big fists clenched and unclenched and
clenched again, in ferocious rhythm.

The Magistrate frowned heavily, and glanced at
Elsa under his brows.   Albrecht Dürer rose.

"Sir Magistrate, I have a witness, in myself, in favor
of the girl.   Since she has abidden in our city she has
done nought but what is right and good."   He seated
himself quietly.

The Magistrate deliberated silently, and then moved
his eyes again toward the bowman.

"What do you know of the object of Herr Grumchen in pursuing this maid?"

The fiery whiskered fellow shuffled his feet uncomfortably, and bellowed confusedly,

"Nay, I know nought. He be a just and a great
wizard, but only for white magic . . . nay, I know
nought save that he pays me to capture his evil spirits,
he pays me well, but no gold did we get for the Lutz
witch till we promised to bring in the girl."

Wilibald Pirkheimer was leaning forward, his chin
in his palm, and his elbow resting on one knee. He
smiled broadly and nodded to Albrecht Dürer,
who bit his lip but said no word. The fingers of the
artist were folding and unfolding the corner of a
paper.

The Magistrate commanded Herr Grumchen to rise.

"What be this your man tells of gold you received?
Who paid you this gold, and for what did you receive
it?"

The face of the witch-hunter grew suddenly yellow
as a sheet of old parchment.

Red Cock thrust out his chin.

"Noble Magistrate," he shouted, "my master be but
trying to catch these evil women. We were not promised much gold, 'twas but—" He stopped suddenly
in confusion and his tongue stuck to the roof of his
mouth. He had caught the eye of his master.

"Herr Grumchen," the Magistrate spoke severely,
"tell us how much gold you were promised, and from
whom?"

The witch-hunter bowed low three times, and his mouth was twisted in a smile.

"Ah, good Magistrate, 'tis right and just that ye should ask. But I swear 'twas but a few batzen which the townsmen gave us for board and lodging, and to pay for my protective ungents and oils."

The weighty voice of the Magistrate filled the room.

"Herr Grumchen, all that you say may be truth. We deny you not your beliefs. But the Magistrate and Council of Nürnberg cannot adjudge guilty a person who has committed no crime in our city. Therefore I do say to you that we cannot punish one for deeds reported done elsewhere."

The dark man stood rigidly. His eyes burned with the flame of marsh fire on a black night. He lifted his hand tightly in a tense slow gesture.

"Master Magistrate, hear me! These be not her only crimes. There be one, and that a grave offense, done here, in the city of Nürnberg, and that right recently."

"What is that?"

Grumchen glanced triumphantly around the room, then fixed his eyes intently on the Magistrate.

"In the house of Nürnberg's master artist the witch-maid, by her magic tricks, got a picture of her evil black cat into a painting, and by this means she spirited away the picture. It was a religious picture, ordered by a lord from Cologne. Herr Dürer can deny not this."

"Nay," spoke the artist slowly, "I say not that the maid took it, whether by magic or otherwise."

"But you can deny not that it be disappeared?"

"Nay, I do not deny that."

The Magistrate's brow grew heavy with concern.

"'Tis bad." He shook his head. "'Tis very bad. 'Tis evidence of withcraft I fear." He frowned heavily at Elsa, "I do conjure you to confess," sternly he spoke to her, "to spit on the floor and say, 'Depart, cursed Devil! I shall do what be just!' "

Hans shuddered convulsively, and Werner, his face white as milk, trembled.

The Magistrate rose from his chair.

"Stop!" cried a harsh voice. All heads turned, amazed, to Frau Agnes, who stood uprightly, her face forbiddingly stern.

"Sir Magistrate, you did not ask for me as a witness, and yet who knows more of this maid than do I, for have I not tried to teach her proper ways since first she came into my house? She be overmuch lazy too, but she did not take the picture. I took it. For I had heard of a rich merchant who was wanting such a one, and he payed me far more for it than that skinflint of a noble offered." Her face flamed a dull red, and seemed near bursting, but she stood defiantly.

Dürer stared, aghast.

"You, Agnes, you took the panel?"

"Yea," she replied angrily, "you are such a fool about gold that I consider it my place to protect you." She drew in her chin obstinately.

Dürer smiled slowly:

"An why, if you took it, do you admit this thing now?"

"'Tis but because I cannot afford to lose another maid, when I have trained this one into my ways." She frowned mightily, as if she dared anyone to suggest that she had any but selfish reasons. There was an amazed silence.

"Then," murmured the Magistrate, "that changes the complexion of this affair. The maid is justified in her blameless reputation in Nürnberg."

The dark man leaned forward, his hands working, his mouth a thin line.

"Know you not that a daughter of a witch always practices the black arts? I be entitled to take her back to Lutz to suffer trial there for her sins."

"You are entitled to do that. An so that is my judgment for Elsa Muller." The Magistrate nodded his head wisely.

Grumchen twisted his lips in a smile. He beckoned to Red Cock, who strode forward and grasped the girl by her arm.

The three ill-assorted figures passed down the hall and had almost reached the door, when the voice of Dürer, strangely loud and commanding, drew them up. Elsa stumbled, and would have fallen save for the tight hold on her arm.

"Stay!" cried the artist, "before you take the maid I wish to read this letter to the Magistrate and the Council. I received it but this morning from the noble who ordered my painting, and who is still at an inn here. I sent him a message saying that I would immediately paint another panel for him, finer than the first, for the same price." He glanced, with a small twinkle in his eye, at his wife, who glared at him.

"An in that message I told him who this witch-hunter was and whence he came.   Here is his answer.

MASTER ALBRECHT DÜRER:

Your offer pleased me well.   I do wish to take advantage of it at once, and will send for the painting in two months' time.   As you say, the disappearance of the first picture is strange, but I think, as do you, that the maid had little to do with it in any magic way, but only as a common thief, in any case.   For it has troubled me, since catching a glimpse of the dark fellow I saw at your doorway, where I had seen him before.   Now I do know. He was whipped from the town of my brother some months agone for maliciously accusing an honest burgess of witchcraft.   This he does, for as much as five hundred gulden, from duped towns-men, in many places.

The artist glanced up at the face of the dark man, which was torn with rage.   The witch-hunter stooped, as if to run from the room.   A soldier hastily moved before the door.   The face of Red Cock swelled until it was the color of his whiskers.   He shook the girl roughly, and loosed his grasp.

Hans stood silent.   He was so confused by the sudden events which trod so rapidly on each others' heels that he hardly knew how things had turned out.   He was staring stupidly at the Magistrate, when Werner nudged him, and whispered joyfully in his ear:

"Ah, Hans, do but see the black fellow.   Master Dürer has confounded him.   Methinks the maid will be troubled with him no more."

The Magistrate stood. His robe extended widely about his knees.

"Bring him to me. And bring the bowman," he commanded.

Two soldiers advanced with the new captives, while the other four remained beside the musicians, not knowing whether their prisoners were still in suspicion or not.

The Magistrate turned to his Council.

"Good fellow townsmen," he said, "do you not all agree with a judgment that these fellows be whipped from the city?"

They nodded solemnly and seriously.

"Herr Grumchen," pronounced the Magistrate, "and Rohte Hahn, this be the final decision. You have defiled our city by maligning an honest girl. Therefore we do say that you both be whipped from the market place through the city to the Frauenthor Gate, and thence into the world. And you be banished forever from this place. This be the judgment of the just city of Nürnberg."

The hall was a still pool. Into the center of it fell the stony voice of Frau Agnes:

"What do ye all mean," she cried, "by keeping a poor maid a-lying on the floor?" She glared at the judge, and turned to the girl, "Elsa," her voice softened a little, "I say ye shall come with me instantly and get ye right into bed for the rest of the day. Say not that ye won't, for I say that ye shall."

CHAPTER XV

SPRING HAS COME

THERE was the first strong scent of spring in the air. Zisselstrasse was no longer covered with white snow, or gray slush, ankle deep. It was dry, and the cobble stones were warm to the feet of children, who played, barefoot, on them, and to the rough hides of dogs which lay about, sleepy and heavy lidded, until obliged to scud across to doorways for safety when an occasional horse galloped through and rounded the corner to the city gate.

Houses, with upper stories like wide brimmed hats to keep out the bright spring sun, opened window eyes and stared solemnly at their neighbors, in like case, across the narrow way. The air was stirred by a little warm breeze, and was filled with the noisy shouts of children, animals and beggars.

Elsa stood in the doorway and looked across at the high frowning wall of the ancient castle, which seemed festive despite its forbidding aspect, for a great lime tree, ages old, in the courtyard, was lifting young green leaves above the wall top. The girl sniffed and smiled, and looked down at Fräulein Bach, who sat demurely on the doorstep.

"Ah," murmured Elsa, "they treat me more like a daughter every day. And now I shall never be afeard of Frau Agnes again, for all her sour ways."

There was a pleasant sound of music coming to her on the small breeze. From the town it came. Ah, it was growing louder.

"Welladay!" smiled the girl, "I must take care, or 'twill tempt me away to the road." But she laughed as she thought of it.

The music turned the corner. Elsa stood, stiff with astonishment. It was made by a musician, in vagabond garments, and he was tall and heavy, and solemn-eyed, and he tooted ever and anon on a zinck, which fitted into a mouth above a crop of curly whiskers. And the eyes above were round and porcelain blue.

Elsa gasped.

"Hans! What means this?"

The broad fellow lifted his instrument from his mouth, and looked a bit sheepish.

"Maid," he rumbled, "I be come to say good-by, for a time."

"But Hans, your fine bakery?"

"'Tis a fine bakery, and that be truthfully said, but the flour chokes my beard, and the warm smell of bread a-baking gives me a pain in the gullet."

"But Hans, ye go not alone, surely?"

"Yea, maid," said the big fellow slowly, "I dare not ask the other two, for Melchior be so wrapped in his bath habits, which he cannot find elsewhere, and Werner be now too fine a Meistersinger to want to take the road."

"Ah, Hans," cried the girl reproachfully, "ye do—"

Hans looked back along the street, and suddenly whispered loudly,

"Hist, that may be Melchior, give me not away to him." He disappeared around the corner, but thrust his round head back to say, "I wait here till he is gone."

Elsa stared in dismay. Coming up the hill was a long lank fellow, dressed in rusty clothes, and around his neck hung a big dudelsack, which was adorned with a monstrous head, whether man or woman or monster she could not tell. He advanced until he stood before her.

"Melchior!" exclaimed the girl, "whence these clothes?"

"Maid," he uttered in a low sad voice, glancing anxiously toward the house as if he expected any minute to see the face of Frau Dürer pop from a window and accuse him of stealing, "maid, I be going away."

"Why go ye without the others?"

"Why," he looked sadly down, "they are at work and liking it too. They will not want to go."

"But, Melchior, why go ye now, when ye were getting as clean as a new scrubbed floor?"

"Yea, 'tis a fine life in the Baths, an-eating and a-gos-siping, but water soaked into me till I were as wrinkled as an old hag.   An I heard so many bath stories till I was a-feared I could tell the truth no more."

"Yea, an can ye now?" asked Elsa with a laugh.

"Yea, but—" he looked down the street, stared in doubt, then he stepped within the doorway.   "Will old sour-face see me an I bide in here a bit?"

"Nay," answered the astonished girl, for she knew that Melchior feared the house like a plague, "she is gone out, but what—"

She had a sudden suspicion, and on the strength of it she craned her neck down toward the city.   A fat, short figure, plump as a new cheese, but covered with old and ragged clothes, came bouncing up to her. And around his neck the fellow had a cither.

"I came to say good-by, maid."

"But Werner, why do ye go?" cried the girl, "for ye be a Meistersinger, an may yet win the golden chain, and a fine cobbler ye be too."

"Yea," spoke Werner, shaking his head as if to cast all doubts from him, "yea, but, devil take me, I pounded my fingers too often while a-tapping on leather, and, may the fiends fly away with me, but I grew weary of the classic and stiff songs, which must be thus," he lapsed into a long, serious face, "and thus," he drew down the corners of his mouth, "and thus," he folded his hands daintily on his middle.

Elsa burst out laughing.

"Confess it, Werner, those are not the reasons?"

"Nay, now that ye say so." He waved his arm in the air, seeming to include the small breeze, the lazy dogs, the frolicsome children, and the faint smell of buds about to burst. "Spring has come. I wander."

"Then," whispered the girl, glancing back at the corner and at the open house door, where the Fräulein sat dozing, "an ye be going, give me one song."

The fat man drew up his cither and struck the strings.

As the notes rolled out, from around the corner came accompanying toots on the zinck. Hans stepped forward. From the doorway came the mournful echoes of music from a dudelsack. Melchior moved out. Werner gave a shout of delight.

Windows popped open suddenly above. Elsa saw a row of shock heads from the journeymen's room. Conrad looked out, and then ran down to join them.

"Ah," cried the youth, "ye are going out to wander again?"

"Yea," rumbled Hans, "an ye and the maid here had better come too."

"And the lively Fräulein," added Werner, pausing.

"Nay," said Conrad, "I go not from this house."

"Nor I either," said Elsa quietly. "But come. I will show ye all why Fräulein Bach cannot go."

She tiptoed softly into the house, followed by the four, in a long procession, across the hall and into the kitchen. In a corner by the stove she pointed to a box. Fräulein Bach ran between the legs of Melchior and leaped in, purring. Four heads leaned over.

There in the box four tiny balls of fur curled around the black cat.

"Ha! She be no longer our Fräulein. She be now Frau Bach."

They went into the street.

"Ach! Fräulein Bach!" murmured Werner.

Elsa sighed. Conrad leaned against the door, and he sighed too. His eyes had a longing gleam, as he saw his comrades prepare to go. The three musicians, with one backward look, took up their instruments, and as they went a song came to the two, borne on the small spring breeze,

"Oh, a restless blade I be, an the end I cannot see.
My home's the spot where I am not. The rough road calls to me."